Chasing A Dream

When the odds are against you…

Novel by
Sheila L Jackson

Virtuous Books

ALSO BY SHEILA L. JACKSON

Non-Fiction

The Enemy Within

Perfectly Normal

Contemporary Christian Novels

Where Was God I
(Big City Lies/Small town Secrets)

Joi and Payne

Where Was God II
(Evil Never Sleeps)

Coming Soon

College Life
Survival of The Fittest

Where Was God III
(When The Tables Turn)

Chasing A Dream
Virtuous Books
Copyright ©2019 Sheila L. Jackson
http://www.sheilaljackson2.com
SJ@comcast.net

Cover Photo By:
selfpubbookcovers.com/BravoCovers
Interior Design: Sheila L. Jackson

ISBN 13:978-1-68411-693-5
ISBN 10:1-68411-693-7

For Worldwide Distribution
Printed in the U.S.A.

DEDICATION

To those who dare to dream. Never give up. Keep on pressing forward, even if you have to take the journey alone.

ACKNOWLEDGEMENTS

Thank you, Lord, for continuing to do great and amazing things through my writing. You taught me that my writing is not about me, but to give light where there is darkness. For without Your anointing, penning, *Chasing A Dream*, would not have been impossible.

To my family and friends who continue to encourage and pray for me, your support means a lot.

I am grateful to the many libraries, churches, and book events in Shreveport, Louisiana and surrounding areas for allowing me to share my gift of writing to the world.

To the bookstores, who never failed to house and set-up my book signing events, thank you so much for your support.

I am always humbled and grateful to the faithful readers who purchased my books. Your e-mails and posts on social media have inspired me to continue to write uplifting material.

Many thanks to those in the ministry, who prayed and encouraged me along the way; this has indeed been a long, hard, and lonely journey. But your interceding for me gives me the strength to persevere.

Chapter 1

With a song in her heart and a desire to one day become a world-class, certified fashion designer, Flo, short for Florence Kinkaid, worked diligently, altering a dress for one of her many loyal customers. Flo Designs and Alteration Shop was a business her husband, William, built adjacent to their home. She loved the thought of being her own boss and never having to deal with the many personalities that came along with working on a 9 to 5 job.

Stitching seam after seam, a smile appeared on Flo's face. Life couldn't get any better than this. She was married to her high school sweetheart for over sixteen years. And as luck would have it, the twin gods managed to strike them twice. She had two sets of twins ranging from five to sixteen-years-old. The older twins, a boy, and girl were fraternal and the younger girls, identical. On her twenty-eighth birthday, she and William felt that their family was complete. They had a son and a daughter, every couple's dream. She had gone to her OB/GYN, Obstetrician-gynecologist, to discuss the options of birth control, only to learn that she was pregnant with not one baby, but two again.

After the final stitch was sown, Flo took a much-needed break to relieve her aching joints. Sitting in the same position for more than an hour had stiffened her muscles. She stretched for a second as her physical therapist recommended for those who worked in the same position for long periods at a time and then poured herself a cup of coffee. A fashion magazine lay opened to a page she was reading earlier. Grabbing it off the table, she relaxed with her legs crossed in a soft recliner in the back room of her shop.

To her surprise, Fashion Week was being held this year in Miami, Florida. The article stated that they were showcasing a new segment where aspiring designers could submit pictures or videos of their designs to take part in the show, if selected. They were choosing five finalists, which was a shock to Flo. In disbelief, she placed her cup on a nearby table and continued reading. Her heart leaped with excitement because she had been waiting for such an opportunity. She finally would get a shot at showing the world greatest designers what she had to offer to the fashion industry, if chosen. On cloud nine, she jumped from her seat in search of an ink pen to fill out the application. She'd dreamt of this moment her entire life and wasn't going to allow the chance to do something great pass her again. Married at an early age and babies a year later prevented her from leaving Gomer, Louisiana to attend one of New York's most prestigious schools of fashion. She'd won a full scholarship after one of the college fashion recruiter's came to her high school to judge and host their fashion show. Now, at thirty-three, she still found herself chasing that same old dream. She tried her best not to focus on the, "what if's," but her heart longed to know if she still had what it took to be among the top designers.

Completing the application was the easy part, but getting the support and encouragement that a wife needed from her husband would take an act of God. William lost himself and the dream of one day starting his own construction company the day they said, "I do." While Flo put her dreams on hold to help raise their children.

~~~~~

The following day, Flo staggered into the kitchen like a zombie, wiping the sleep from her eyes to start another busy day as a seamstress. She fumbled her hand against the wall in search of the light switch. Like a stunned deer, the bright light slapped the sleep straight from her eyes. It was Tuesday morning, time for her to start the same old daily routine of making William and the kids' breakfast and packing his lunch. Her four kids were snuggled in their beds; getting the rest and sleep she wished she had the luxury of getting. After reading and filling out the fashion competition application the previous day, she realized that there was more to life than fulfilling everyone else's needs while hers go unmet.

Flo never knew what it meant to live alone. She left her parents' home to live with her new husband in a small, one bedroom apartment. That was what people did in the small town of Gomer, Louisiana. Get a job after high school, marry, and start a family. There was no honeymoon because they were practically kids themselves who had no money. Both their parents' made it perfectly clear that grown folks needed their own place. So, William found a job in construction which he has done ever since. It provided a great life for them and he made sure that she and the kids needed or wanted for nothing.

William, the definition of what a real man was supposed to be. His spirited nature was what brought them together. And it didn't hurt that he was tall, handsomely, solid built, and played on the varsity football team in high school. He took great care of his family. The way a man should. Working in construction brought an added bonus to their love life. His calloused hands sent goose bumps unrestrainedly up and down her body each time he touched her. But somewhere down the years, he'd become more focused on his job as a foreman at the construction plant and earning a hefty retirement package to help secure them in their old age, that he'd lost sight of his dream. He'd always wanted to open his own construction company and could reconstruct or build from scratch anything he imagined. Her alteration shop was a testament to that. No business of her kind in Gomer, Louisiana, could compare to the one William built for her.

Flo loved her family but wondered at times if they thought the same for her. They were blessed and didn't know it. Most women could care less if their families' needs were met or not. She'd lost herself somewhere down the years by waiting on them hand and

6

foot. Her teenagers only snuggled up to her when they needed money or to extend their curfew on a school night. The five-year-olds were little terrors in their father's absence but behaved like angels in his presence.

Flo pulled the skillet from under the cabinet and began cooking breakfast for her husband and kids. Her heart sulked at the thought that no one ever cooked her breakfast while she lied in bed. In their minds, it was her job to take care of them, but she was beginning to grow tired of it and knew that things had to change. Her job as a seamstress may not seem important to them, but it brought her joy. They didn't consider sewing for a living was real work, but her aching back and neck said differently.

Thankfully, she had great friends to confide in or else she would have lost her mind or worse, gave up on her dream. Naydean, Louisa, and Kennedy were childhood friends. Marriage, careers, and difference in opinions could never destroy their friendship. They kept each other sane throughout the years. Recently, when the yearning began to stir in her spirit to pursue a career as a designer, she confided in her girlfriends, knowing William wouldn't entertain the thought.

He was a great husband, but the years had worn him down. He'd lost the enthusiasm of exploring what life had to offer. His dream of owning a business died each time their family grew. But Flo refused to allow her aspirations to go to the great graveyard in the sky. She had plans of getting her designs sold online, and then in department stores. She was great. No, take that back, she was gifted. God had given her an eye for detail and mad skills on a sewing machine.

Wet lips pressed against her cheeks as she pressed the button to start the coffee maker. "Hey Bae," William greeted in a deep, groggy voice, looking over at the empty table. "Good morning," she turned, giving him a weak peck on the lips. She had gotten a late start on preparing his breakfast today. She had several dresses to make since it was prom season and was just as tired as he. Waiting a few minutes on his food wasn't going to kill him. With shoulders slumped, he strode to the table and took a seat. Watching him from behind in his work pants, Flo couldn't help but admire how working in construction kept him in great shape over the years. As hard as it was, a smile managed to make its way to her lips in appreciation.

"You know I don't have long, Flo, before I have to get to work." He buried his face in the palms of his hands as his elbows rested on top of the table.

She cut her eyes over at him. If only he knew what she was thinking.

Moments later, before he could utter another word, she placed his food and a glass of orange juice and coffee in front of him, which brought a smile to his chiseled face. Only the smile wasn't for her. William was a big man who loved to eat and food always made him happy.

"Here you go. Eat up." She returned to the stove and covered up the remaining food for the kids when they awake for school.

She took a seat beside her husband and brought up the same complaint she'd had for the last several years. She wanted to go on a vacation. Some place far. William considered Dallas, Texas, a get-a-away trip, but it was only when the Dallas Cowboys played a home game that they traveled there. He just didn't get it. She wanted to go somewhere exciting, exotic, and romantic.

"William, we need to get away, just the two of us," she said, seductively, staring at him chomping down on his food. He never looked up at her, making her feel some type of way. "There is a life outside of Gomer, you know."

Chewing in rapid motion, he commented, "People are going crazy with these mass shootings and driving trucks with bombs into crowds, baby. We need to wait until things get better, then we'll see the world."

She rolled her eyes, tired of hearing the same old yadda, yadda.

"And besides, we can't afford it right now." He pushed his plate forward, sucked his teeth, and said, "Are you going through...um, what they call it?"

She cut her eyes over at him, annoyed, knowing what he was about to say.

"A mid-life crisis."

"Are you serious, Will? It's been years since the two of us have gone anywhere alone. And no, I'm not going through a mid-life crisis. I'm tired of coming in last place in this house."

She stood from her seat, hands on hip, continuing her complaint.

"It's bad enough that I've had to put my dreams on hold. And so have you." She didn't mean for that to slip out, but his cheapskate ways made her lash out and say what she'd been holding in.

"Look, I have to go." He pushed from the table, wiping his mouth. He tried leaning in to kiss her goodbye.

She winced, turning her face away from him.

He tried once more to touch her but she remained stiff as a board. "Flo, we're not kids anymore and we're certainly not getting any younger. It's time we let go of these pipe dreams."

She gasped with her hand clasped against her chest, hurt by the sting of his words, "Pipedreams." Her voice quivered. "As long as God continues to breathe life into my body, I will never lose faith in the gift He has given me." Without warning, tears welled up in her eyes. "I want more out of life than just taking care of you and the kids."

The bass rose in his voice. "So, what are you saying, Flo? That this life isn't good enough for you anymore? I provide a good life for us. I don't understand what your problem is."

In a blank stare, she said, "Never mind. You just don't get it. And you never will." She waved him off and left the room. True, he was a great provider, but she wanted to pave her own path. What sense did it make to live and never at least try? There was more to her than just being William Kinkaid's wife and the mother of his four children. She was a woman with purpose.

Like many other men and women who became successful later on in life by never listening to the naysayers, she had to do the same. Whether William thought it made sense or not, she couldn't give up without a try. They were always encouraging their kids to never allow anything or anyone stop them. But they were hypocrites, because they were doing exactly what they taught against.

Chapter 2

Taken aback by her and William's conversation earlier at breakfast, she wandered into her bedroom, closed the door, and fell backward onto the bed. How could he be so dead-set against her wanting to be more than just the neighborhood seamstress? His words cut her to the quick when he suggested that she may be menopausal. It would have been a slap in the face to any woman's ego. Wrestling with how to handle the situation later once he returns home from work, her five-year-old twins came crashing through the door and jumped in bed beside her.

"Mama, mama, mama," they sang while tangling themselves up in the covers. "We're hungry."

What she wanted to do was stay closed up in her bedroom and sulk about not using her God-given gift. But like a good mother, she said, "Come on. Let mama fix her babies something to eat."

They jumped out the bed like good little soldiers, running down the hallway, and then into the kitchen. Before she could step foot inside, Julia and William Jr. sat at the table, waiting on their maid to serve them. What she should have done years earlier was to make them more responsible. She thought it was sweet in the beginning, the thought of feeling needed by everyone. Now, it was getting on her nerves. She should have given them chores and made them earn their allowances. As they grew older, she'd hoped that something would have clicked in their minds or even taken the intuitive to help out. But the only thing clicking was the buttons on their cellphones. Although it angered Flo, she knew that she played a part in handicapping her kids.

The older twins had the nerves to sit at the kitchen table like two-years-old, waiting for her to serve them. They were more than capable of preparing their own breakfast. No one took into account that she worked just as hard as their father, although what she did for a living wasn't considered real work. On the other hand, her five-year-olds were too young to fend for themselves, but they took the initiative to set their own plates on the table and pour themselves a cup of milk. Too bad her oldest couldn't take a hint.

With her working near home, it saved money on child care and afforded her the luxury of being her own boss. Occasionally, she did have to hire someone to babysit her youngest kids when the shop became bogged down with orders. Her eldest twins were active in after-school activities and busy social lives to help. William never wanted to put their kids into daycare because of some of the horror stories aired on the evening news.

"It's time the two of you start helping out around the house," Flo voiced while serving them breakfast. "You are old enough to clean up behind yourselves. I'm tired of you thinking that I'm your live-in maid, instead of your mother."

As usual, they stared at her as if she were speaking a foreign language. When she placed the food on the table, their hearing went out of the window. Hands were reaching at biscuits, bacon, and eggs. Flo swore an octopus had invaded her kitchen.

"William Jr, Julia, did the two of you hear me? Today is the last day that I will be preparing breakfast for your overgrown behinds," she announced, patting her foot on the floor, waiting for a response.

Quickly, their heads lifted from their plates, eyes enlarged in their sockets.

"I knew that would get your attention.

"Are you serious?" William Jr. asked. His deep voice rose as he dropped his fork into his plate. No doubt, he was shocked by the news that he'd just heard, to start doing his fair share around the house. "I have a life. I don't have time for chores."

Placing her hand on her hip, Flo responded, "I see you have time to slap your butt into that chair and swallow down the food that my tired hands have prepared. Well then, you got time to contribute some help around here."

What she wanted to do was knock him upside the head. Who did he think she was, Florence from the Jefferson? If she could go back in time, she would have stopped fixing their plates for them much earlier. At least with her babies, she had the chance to do things differently.

Princess Julia finally opened her mouth to speak after mumbling under her breath when Jr. voiced his displeasure of the new rules. "But you are our mother. You are supposed to take care of us."

Twirling one of her braids around her finger as if her statement was going to change her mind, made Flo more determined to enforce her new rules. Julia's long lashes batting up at her with a childlike innocence made Flo growled. She wasn't going to be suckered in by those big brown eyes of hers. The mood she was in today made her wanted to snatch both their plates from in front of them. Her family Julia might play her father with that routine but not her. It was time she put her foot down. Their lack of help and taking responsibility for themselves was taking away the time she needed to draw up new designs. Her family couldn't see it now, but things were about to change in their home. Either they were going to get on board or be forced. Their selfish ways would no longer be tolerated.

"I'm going to be a dead mother if I don't get some help around here," she yelped at them both. The looks on their faces told her that they weren't taking her seriously, but when they awake to a cold stove in the morning, it would jog some sense into their heads.

"What about me and Landon mama," London whined, looking over at her twin.

Landon shrugged her shoulders at her and then turned her attention back to Flo. "Is that true, mama?" She placed her fork down and began to pout, looking over London to do likewise. They were identical in every sense of the word.

She walked to where they were seated and said, "No baby. I'm talking to those grown folks over there." Of course, that didn't sit well with William Jr. and Julia but asked if she cared. If they wanted to act grown, then they were going to do grown folk chores.

The twins let out a high-pitched scream that almost burst her eardrums. "Yeahhhhhhhhh, we still get to eat." They looked over at their brother and sister and licked their tongues out at them and began to laugh.

"Alright you two, stop teasing your brother and sister."

"Yeah stop. Before I come over there," Jr. threatened, while balling his fist at them.

"And do what?" Landon sat up on her knees in the chair to appear taller.

"You don't scare us," London snapped, now on her knees in the chair, pointing over at him.

As usual, Julia was in her own world, texting. The bickering between her siblings seemed to go unnoticed.

"Don't forget who takes the two of you to school." His brows lowered, a smirk rose to his lips.

"And don't you forget we went through your text messages." London folded her arms, giving him a cold hard stare down. Of course, Landon did the same.

"We know what you did last Friday," Landon said as she and her sister high-fived each other.

"Enough," Flo stopped them before they could go any further. What did he do last Friday? "All of you go and get ready for school. Earth to Julia." She waved a hand in front of her daughter's face to distract her from her cellphone. "Take your brother and sister and help them get dressed.

Flo could tell from the look on her face that Julia wasn't happy about the command she was given. Today, Flo was implementing some new rules, starting with making her lazy teenagers pull their weight around the house. Far too long she had been passive in that area.

When the kids left the kitchen, Flo flopped down into one of the chairs with a cup of coffee in hand. She allowed her mind to take her to a peaceful place. Quickly, reality interrupted, causing her to face the truth about where she went wrong in raising her teenagers.

Maybe if she and William had taken more parental control when they were younger, things would be different. When they were little, everything Julia and Jr. did seem adorable. Their innocent faces made it hard to disciple them. Now, she regretted her and William's leniency toward them. They have created lazy and selfish teenagers.

Flo wished that Julia shared her passion for sewing, but she was too busy chasing boys and the varsity cheerleading squad took up most her time. The first time she held her in her arms, she dreamt of them being a mother and daughter designer team. That image quickly faded when Julia turned twelve and told her she never liked sewing and that she only did it to make her happy. Hearing her daughter utter those words crushed her to the

Since things didn't go the way she had planned, Julia as her assistant. Flo had to hire teens or adults looking to make some extra cash to help her around the shop when she had large orders to fill. Her assistants had to have former training when it came to sewing, which helped her to deliver to the local boutiques on time. The owners allowed her to showcase her designs for a small fee, which was reasonable. The chance for locals to wear her outfits, made her name spread around town. Many outsiders passing through wondered who Flo Style Fashions was. Her sales increased because of those boutiques willing to carry her clothes.

Flo stopped her internal whining long enough and head over to the counter to pour herself another cup of coffee, hoping it would give her the boost she needed to get her day started. She heard the kids yelling that they were leaving for school. The twins ran back into the kitchen and gave her a hug and kiss, which brought a smile to her face. She remembered when her eldest kids did the same. Now, there were no hugs, kisses or, goodbyes from them.

"Bye mommy," they sang in unison. "We love you."

Their backpacks were almost as big as them as it hung on the small frames.

"I love the both of you too." She kissed them and sent them on their way after hearing Julia shouting for them to hurry up. She released them from her arms and said, "Go on before your sister wake the entire neighborhood with all that shouting."

They stormed down the hallway, slamming the door behind them. "Good, now I can have some peace and quiet." She took a sip of her coffee, still trying to get inspired to head out to her shop. The application stated that each winner had to bring their unique designs and sketches to Miami with them. For that to happen, she had to start working on something now, as if she'd already been selected. If she wasn't chosen, then she could always sell the designs in one of the local stores or boutiques.

The silence and the coffee got her creative juices flowing. She ran to her bedroom closet and grabbed her sketch pad and pencil. She then allowed the Holy Spirit to move as only He could within her. She headed back into the kitchen where she'd left her coffee and sat at the table. Her hand danced across each page gracefully as she worked her magic. Images flashed in her mind as she captured the essence of each one.

Within a couple of hours, she had several sketches to choose from if she was picked as one of the five finalists. Now, all she had to do was create a pattern, select what type of fabric and color she wanted for each, and then the sewing began. She felt accomplished despite the ruckus she'd experienced earlier that day.

The morning had turned into noon and she still wore her bathrobe. It didn't seem to matter because God had blessed her with what she thought would've taken weeks to create. She flipped through each page with a feeling of great satisfaction.

Chapter 3

Large hands ran through her natural coils as she lay face to face on a pillow she shared with her husband. Wet, hungry, and passionate lips pressed against hers as he held her close, making her feel things that only a husband could. His calloused hands sent tingles down her spine as he caressed her bare skin.

William was the only man she'd ever known intimately and the love he had given her over the years, never once made her second-guess that she should have sown her wild oats before getting married. As his hands traveled in familiar places, forgiveness overshadowed the hurt. The way he was making her feel erased every negative thought she had earlier. His touch had the ability to do that. Somehow, he'd managed to get back into her good graces before the sun had set.

"Mmm,mmm,mmm," she purred in his arms as his lips traveled from her mouth to her neck. Her hands cradled the back of his head, guiding it over her body. The weight of his body covered hers as they became one to the sounds of their love.

"I love you, baby," William whispered in her ear, and then covered her mouth with his.

The way they were coupled together tonight, she wished they could be connected when it came to their outlook on life. William placed her hands over her head, locking his fingers through hers. He gave her all the love he had inside. It made her feel that there was no other place she'd rather be than underneath him.

Calmness washed over them as they panted from the special moment they'd just shared with each other. He eased off her and scooped her up into his arms, holding her tight. With him being in such a serene mood,

Flo wanted to continue their conversation from earlier, but she didn't want to ruin what they'd just shared. It didn't matter if she'd wanted to or not. William's loud snoring alerted her that he'd fallen asleep.

Nestled in his arms, she craned her neck up at her sleeping husband and wondered how a man that was so intelligent and gifted with his hands could be so clueless when it came to matters of the heart.

Tired of hearing her husband's loud, thunderous snores, she joined him in a sweet, peaceful rest.

The next day, William rose early to find his wife still asleep. With a smile on his face, he stared at her angelic features, sleeping like a baby. One fact was true; he was a blessed man. He and Flo had survived many ups and downs in their marriage when most of their friends had thrown in the towel, filing for divorce.

In the past, their young relationship had been tainted by lies, jealousy, and lust, which almost tore them apart. His arrogance and entitlement as a star quarterback had his head in the clouds. Girls practically threw themselves at him. His flesh was weak and wanted to try every color of the rainbow when it came to women. Flo knew when they became a couple that he had been with other girls when she'd confessed being a virgin. At first, he didn't think that he could be with someone so innocent and pure, but she made him a better person. She showed him that life was more than just sleeping around and hanging with the wrong crowd to be popular. The woman lying next to him taught him what it meant and took to be a real man.

When Flo left him after an ex-girlfriend lied that they were still seeing each other, he almost lost his mind. After their two-month hiatus, Flo began dating someone else which caused him to see red. Never in his life had he loved any girl the way he loved Flo. She had goals and ambitions and knew who she was as a young woman. The girls he used to date had no plans in life other than dating whoever was popular at that moment.

William brushed his hands through his wife's delicate curls, and then swept his thumb against her almond smooth skin. The thought of losing her sent shivers up his spine. Lately, she'd seemed detached from him, he even felt it last night when they were intimate. He nearly lost her years ago to another man and would fight a grizzly bear to keep from losing her now. When he witnessed another man kissing Flo after school, he ran upon them and tried to provoke a fight with the guy. It hurt William even more because the guy was of another race. He knew he had no right to be judgmental, seeing that he had been with girls outside of his race, but Flo was his soulmate. They were destined to be together.

He caressed her shoulder as she stirred in her sleep. William swore she was the most beautiful woman in the world. Most times, he'd failed to tell her that. Maybe that was why she seemed distant. He worked himself to the bone to make sure that she was happy. He'd give her the world if it was in his power to do so, just to see the sparkle in her eyes again. He'd tried his best to read her mind but he just couldn't put his finger on why she appeared so discontent, lately.

What if she was interested in another man? He closed his eyes tight, ridding himself of that thought. Flo was a godly woman, she would never cheat on him, but yet, the thought still lingered in the back of his mind.

He nestled close to her, to feel the warmth and softness of her body. Whatever it took to keep her happy, he would do because their lives were perfect as it was. He couldn't see what needed fixing. He was more than happy with his life. He was married to the most gorgeous woman in Gomer, which many envied.

At five-foot-nine and a figure that still turned heads, she continued to take his breath away. One thing that he was thankful for, Flo took excellent care of herself and jogged every afternoon with her girlfriends.

Without realizing it, he held her so tight that he woke her up. "Baby, you are squeezing me too hard," she moaned.

Quickly easing his grip, he said, "Sweetie, I'm so sorry. I didn't mean to wake you."

He lied. William wanted to finish what they started last night. It was early in the morning. The kids were tucked in their beds and he needed to be with his wife.

"That's okay," she uttered through a yawn.

Acting on impulse, William went to her side of the bed and scooped her up in his arms. The thought of her losing interest in him made him feel the need to prove himself.

"William. What are you doing?" she asked, trying to wipe the sleep from her eyes.

"I want you to come and take a shower with me." He smiled down at her, hoping that she'd accept his offer.

"What time is it?" she asked, craning her neck around him to see the clock. "It's six in the morning."

"And?" he smiled, brushing his lips against hers. She had a way of setting his insides on fire by just staring into those mesmerizing, brown eyes of hers. "Remember when we used to get up earlier than this to be together."

She tossed her head back in his arms and smiled. "What if the kids come knocking on the door?"

"That's what locks are for," he said, making his way into the bathroom with her in tote.

"But it's still so early and I have to get several orders delivered today."

"I'm not taking no for an answer." Before she could utter another word, they were inside the master bathroom. She slid out of his arms as he turned on the shower, pulling her inside with him.

Water trickled down her toned body as she asked, "What has gotten into you, Will?"

"You." He raked his thumb against her lips. "I love you, baby. And I want you to know that I appreciate you."

He leathered her silky skin from top to bottom. He loved how the water made her natural curls fall around her neck. He brushed them back with his hand and pinned her back against the shower wall and showed her how much he really loved her.

Chapter 4

A month later, Flo hurried to the mailbox. The application she'd filled out from the fashion magazine was due to arrive. With urgency, she snatched opened the door to their brick mailbox. She squealed out loud when she pulled out the long-awaited package from Loran Sinclair. It was rumored on social media that Ms. Sinclair only sent those who were selected a personally addressed letter. Flo prayed that it was true. Halfway up the driveway, curiosity got the better of her. She tore open the thick package and pulled out a handful of papers with instructions. Careful not to overlook the slightest of details, she ran into the house so neighbors wouldn't think that she had lost her mind. Flo's eyes moved like a snail as her finger followed along each line. Her hands shook and legs became too weak to stand from the anticipation. She grabbed one of the chairs from the kitchen table and collapsed in it. In her heart, she knew that this was her time, her season, and her breakthrough.

Once she finished reading the letter, Flo thanked and praised God for His blessing and giving her the opportunity to finally get her designs seen by one of the biggest designers in New York City. Loran Sinclair was holding her next event in Miami, Florida. There, she would search for the next two designers from among the five finalists and one of them could possibly be her. She could see it now, super-models, gracing the catwalk in her designs. It all seemed surreal, but the acceptance letter in her hand was proof that her life was about to change in a new direction.

Lately, William had been satisfying her every physical need, but she needed more, his support, for starters. Sewing wasn't something she did as a pastime, like he believed. Instead of trying to convince him about how serious she was, she shutdown and stopped talking about it altogether. But holding it in only made her felt worst. She wanted her life partner to be a part of her new journey.

Her head spun in disbelief as she searched the messy table for her cellphone and speed dialed her friends. She wanted to call William first, but she didn't want him to go ruining her good mood with his negative words. She didn't know when, why, or how, William became so complacent with his life. He was once the most outgoing man she knew, but somewhere down the line, he'd lost his zing. His excuse had always been, he had a family to take care of or the bills weren't going to pay themselves. It was hard getting him to see that it was possible to have it all, the family, the careers they always longed for.

With much soul searching, she decided to call one of her best friends since childhood, Louisa. Out of her three friends, she was the most level-headed one. She told it as she saw it. If it didn't make sense or felt right, she wasn't the one to mince words.

On the other hand, Kennedy loved herself and men, in that order. Wherever they were, so was she. When discussing a serious matter with her, the conversation always led back to men.

Naydean was the conservative one. When the preacher mentioned those members who were so heavenly-bound that they were no earthly good, well, she fitted the description. She wouldn't know what fun was if it slapped her in the face. She was the one who found fault in others when her flaws stared her dead in the face. Let's not talk about the way she dressed. Flo has tried on many occasions to create a new wardrobe that was in the twenty-first century. She wouldn't dare wear a skirt or dress above the knee. A sleeveless shirt was out of the question. She'd find a sweater or jacket to cover her arms. Most times, her blouses would conceal the length of her beautiful swan-like neck.

"Hey, gi-rr-rr-l. I got some exciting news!" Flo shouted through the phone."

Before Flo could tell her the good news, she yelled, "You got the letter, didn't you?"

Louisa's joy spilled over in her voice.

"How did you know?" Sounding throaty from the screaming and shouting she'd done before calling. "I just got the news."

"I knew you could do it," she paused, "I'm so proud of you."

"I haven't been this happy in a long time. As far as it relates to my career. I've tried to keep the faith for so long and now," she gulped, "It has paid off."

"Have you told Naydean and Kennedy yet?"

"No, not yet. I'm going to call them later."

"What about William?"

Dead silence.

Flo heard what only a true friend could hear in the other's voice and that was, concern.

"I will tackle that situation when he gets home tonight." Her heart sunk, knowing she didn't have his support. Flo knew that he would only try to talk her from going to

Miami. He'd claim how he and the kids needed her at home. This time, she wasn't yielding to his irrational thinking. In his mind, William believed that he fulfilled her every need. Her wanting to become someone other than everyone's caretaker didn't mean she was unhappy being his wife and mother to their kids.

"He'll come around, just tell him."

"I don't know, Louisa. But if he decides not to come with me to Miami, then the three of you better start saving your money because we are going to make this a girls' trip."

"Are you listening to yourself, Flo," alarm sounded in her voice. "So, you're seriously going to go without William even if he says, no?"

"Yes, I'm not going to turn down this opportunity just because he's stuck in his ways. Who knows where this could lead to?" She toyed with the salt and pepper shaker on the table, scared of what her decision might do to her marriage. "I pray he goes with me, but if not. Yes, I'm willing to leave without him."

"As much as I would love to go to Miami, where they have some of the finest men, I pray that William supports you on this one."

They laughed but Flo weakly.

"I hope so too. And besides, you're married, what do you know about fine men?"

"I'm not blind. I still enjoy glancing a time or two at something yummy. Marriage hasn't dulled my attraction to the opposite sex." A loud laugh escaped her lips. "Just wait until you get down there, you will say, William who, when one of those tight bodies stroll your way."

Louisa's laugh was infectious, which Flo needed a distraction. "I better go. I need to practice what I'm going to say to William later tonight," she moaned, thinking about the outcome.

Louisa yelled, "Practice! Heck, just tell him."

Flo said her goodbyes and disconnected the call. She knew how Louisa could get worked up when she thought that Flo was being silly, but she was right. There was only one way to do it and that was to tell him. If he said no and tried discouraging her from going, she'd decide her next move then.

⟶

William walked through the door worn down from a hard day's work. Flo met him at the door, something she'd never done without cause and he knew it. She took the lunch box from his hand, kissed him on the cheeks, and then led him down the hallway to the master bathroom.

Suspicion shone in his eyes. William was no fool and frankly, she didn't care what he thought at that moment. Her only concern was going to Miami with his blessing.

She had bribed her sixteen-year-olds to take the babies out for pizza and a movie, in exchange for an extra hour added to their weekend curfew. Needless to say, they both jumped for the chance to stay out late with their friends.

Once she pushed open the bathroom door, William stared down at her and asked, "What do you want, Flo?" He sounded tired as he blocked the entrance with his long arms, treading with caution.

Flo rehearsed the entire day how she was going to tell William her good news. Hoping that with the letter, he'd acknowledge that a career in fashion wasn't a 'so-called' pipedream. For some strange reason, a sense of courage swelled up inside of her. Then out of her mouth came a voice, sounding foreign to her.

"I am going to Miami, Florida," she stated, her words chasing after the other.

"You are?" he asked, apparently surprised by her sudden news flash. "That's news to me."
"Yes, I am." She pulled the winning letter from her pocket to show him. Hoping that it sparked some type of reaction, but it didn't. "I have been chosen as one of the finalists to

attend the Loran Sinclair's Fashion week next month." She continued to stand her ground.

"Are you still on that kick?" He unblocked the doorway, shaking his head.

Her eyes lowered and heart sank in disappointment.

He continued, "You are too old and have too many responsibilities around here to keep trying to chase after some dream that is not going to come true. I'm just trying to save you from the hurt and shame that will follow when it doesn't work out."

Those words slapped the wind from her lungs. Tears filled her eyes but she wasn't going to back down this time. She gathered her composure and let in on him. "I'm going to Miami. You can stay here in Gomer, Louisiana, and dry up but not me." She stood tall, staring up at him with nostrils blazing. "When has thirty-three years of age been considered ancient? You're unhappy with your job but afraid to walk in faith and try something new and different. I'm not like you."

In his eyes shone fear staring back at her. What was he so afraid of? Before she could turn and walk away, he grabbed her by the arm. His voice softened. "Flo, all I'm saying is that we're not getting any younger. The money we have saved is to secure us in our golden years and put the kids through college. I can't risk losing everything we've worked hard to build on a whim."

"Are you listening to yourself, Will? You're saving for a day that may never come. Tomorrow is not promised to any of us." What was it going to take to knock some sense into this man?

"Say what you want Flo, I'm not going to jeopardize our money for no fantasy." He released her arm and stepped inside the bathroom, leaving her standing at the door. Anger surrounded her as she watched him remove his clothes to shower without her. The conversation may be over for him, but it wasn't for her.

"I have already booked my fight. I'm going with or without you." She shouted over the sound of the running water, slamming the door behind her.

Flo stormed down the hallway, called her friends to book their flights to Miami, and then made plans for her mother-in-law to watch the twins in her absence. Thankfully, William's mother was a jewel. She'd even made one-of-a-kind outfit for her when she wanted to impress the other ladies at her church on special occasions. When they'd ask where she'd purchased her dresses, Isabella bragged that her daughter, "the fashion designer," made them just for her.

Her plans were set in motion. The hard part was deciding what to wear. If she wanted to impress the judges and Loran Sinclair, she'd have to look as if she belonged in Miami.

Minutes later, William emerged from the bathroom, as if nothing had happened, wrapping his arms around her waist and bringing his negative aura back into her space.

"I hope you have calmed down from this nonsense about going to Florida?" he asked, kissing her on the neck.

She elbowed him in the gut and removed his arms that used to bring her so much comfort and peace. "When did you become this negative person? I don't recognize who you are anymore."

He held her by the shoulders to keep her from leaving, while still trying to enforce his nonsense on her. "Who am I? Who are you? You want to travel halfway around the world...and for what? To live a childhood fantasy?"

"A childhood fantasy?" she shouted, knocking his hands off her shoulders. "William, There is so much to see and do out there. You can ball up and die without seeing it, if you want to but not me."

"You have your own alteration shop with plenty of business. Isn't that enough?"

He stared down at her, clueless of how his words had stung.

William just wasn't getting it. The only way for him to see that she was serious about becoming more than just the neighborhood seamstress was to go out and do it. It was apparent that her words weren't registering with him. "This conversation is over." Flo tried pushing pass him, but he held on to her. She knew what that move implied but getting her between the sheets wasn't happening tonight. His belittling her career choice has put him in the doghouse for a very long time. How could she be intimate with a man that doesn't have faith in her vision?

"Good," he said smiling down at her with that look in his eyes. "I thought since the kids were out, we could have a little fun ourselves."

Sadly, he didn't realize that he had ruined her mood. How could she think about romance when he'd torn her heart out? He'd made her feel that she was incapable of making a level headed decision on her own.

She shot him a nasty look and left him standing in their bedroom with nothing but a towel wrapped around his waist. She had to admit, the offer sounded tempting. His hard rock, glistening abs made her unable to think straight, but she had to stay strong or he would think that all he had to do was show some skin and she'd fold on his command.

Chapter 5

The rain trickled down the bedroom window like the tears down Flo's sodden cheeks. On any given morning, she'd been out of bed, dressed, and in her shop working on her next creation. Today, she felt as gloomy as the clouds looked in the sky. Still sulking from William's words the previous night, she didn't have the strength to peel herself from under her plush covers.

Commotions could be heard through the bedroom door, warning her that everyone was upset that no breakfast was waiting for them on the table. She heard their cries, but this time, she refused to go running to their beck and calls.

As far as she was concerned, each of them could take care of themselves, even her babies. Although they were five-years-old, they were tall enough to reach for a box of cereals from the counter and the milk, which she kept on the bottom shelf of the refrigerator. What she should have never done was coddle them, which in doing so, made them unable to take care of themselves. Now, she wanted the madness she'd created to stop. She kept her body facing the opened window, wishing she could will herself someplace else today as she drowned out her family cries.

Flo continued to relive the pain she'd held inside all those years of never leaving Gomer, Louisiana, to move to New York. She'd felt a lot better if she had tried, at least, she wouldn't have any regrets.

A handful of the church mothers agreed with William about her age and that caring for her family took precedence over a career. Sadly, most African Americans' visions dimmed if they haven't become all that they wanted to be by twenty-nine years of age. Why was it so wrong for her to want it all? She never understood why her culture put an age limit on achieving goals in their lives. On the other hand, her counterparts would follow their dreams, even to the grave. Today, amid the cloudy skies, Flo decided to do the same, keep the faith until something happens.

Her body stiffened by the sound of the bedroom door opening. She knew it was William checking on her before he left for work. Today, she was in no mood to deal with him. Like most insensitive males, he had no clue that his words had hurt her deeply.

"Flo... baby, are you awake?" he whispered, tip-toeing toward the bed.

She kept silent, hoping that he would leave, but he didn't. Flo could never understand how the love of her life could dismiss her feelings, but yet sensitive when it came to taking care of her physical needs and making sure that she was well. She closed her eyes and pretended to be in a deep sleep. He came around to face her. His face was so close that she could smell the bacon on his breath, which told her that they were more than capable of taking care of themselves. Wet lips pressed against her forehead, and then he turned and left the room, easing the door shut behind him.

Her eyes popped open as soon as she heard the door close, which meant that he was leaving for work and the kids had left for school. Like a thunderous roar, thoughts rolled through her mind of how her life had become so unfulfilled and complacent.

Out of nowhere, an outpouring of inspiration shot through her. Flo tossed the covers off. Like superwoman, she was ready to take on the challenges of the day. Her eyes landed over to her laptop. Soon, her clouds faded when she ran and logged on to it. She strolled through her emails and found the second acceptance letter from the competition. She replied that she would be attending. In doing so, they would send hotel reservations and flight tickets for two passengers. Thankful they were given options for room reservations, she asked for a suite that could sleep four.

At noon, Flo's friends came over to discuss their trip to Miami. As usual, Kennedy came swaying her hips through the door in her heels and skin-tight mini-shirt. It didn't matter if a man was around or not, she had to always look her best. Her reason was; she was on the prowl for husband number four. Behind her came Naydean and Louisa, fussing about something. Knowing Naydean, she probably was preaching to them on the way over.

"Hello, ladies," Flo greeted, smiling from ear to ear. Her spirits had lifted since this morning. "I'm glad you all showed up at a decent time."

"Girl, when you said that we were going to Miami," Kennedy said, wagging her head from side to side, "That put some steam in my behind to rush over."

They laughed, agreeing.

"Mmm mmm mmm," Louisa moaned, sniffing toward the kitchen. "Something smells scrumptious."

"Oooooo, sure does," Naydean said, trailing the others into the kitchen.

"I made you all's favorite...chicken spaghetti, rolls, and salad. Because had I told you to come over and there was no food, ya'll hungry behinds would have talked about me behind my back."

"And you know that's the truth," Kennedy shouted.

The ladies chatted as they fixed their plates and drinks and headed to the outside patio area to discuss their trip. Flo understood it was a trip for pleasure for her friends, but for her, it was business Taking a bold move such as this would make those that made little of her ambitions stand up and take notice or blow completely up in her face.

From the way they were choking down their food, Flo thought they would never get around to discussing their trip. She wanted to get everything sorted out before William and the kids return home. The last thing she needed to hear was more disapproving talk.

Even in high school, there were those rooting against her when she won first place in home economics, as the best designer of that class.

To get the ball rolling, Flo stood from her seat to get her friends to put down their folks long enough to make plans for their trip. Most times they visited for hours, but today, she needed to get them in and out as quickly as possible. Although William's mom had been informed about her plans, they agreed to keep quiet about her leaving within a week, which expressed her urgency of finishing up their meeting.

"Girls, I've booked our room in Miami. But I need to know before next week, are you serious about going?" She propped against the chair.

With eagerness in her voice, Kennedy spoke up for them. "Heck yeah, we're serious.

We just stopped by to get a free lunch before going back to the salon to work."

The three own a beauty salon together, which meant being together six days a week.

"Girl, we're booking heads like crazy at the salon to get our coins together," Louisa snapped her fingers and smiled. "Can we say, Cha-Ching?"

Even Naydean, with her overly conservative ways, chimed in on the matter. "I have never been outside of Gomer. So you know I'm going." She crossed her hands on the table like an old woman at a tea party.

"Naydean," Kennedy said, "I mean this in the best way possible because you are like a sister to me. Please go out and buy a whole new wardrobe before we leave town. I do not want you embarrassing us with those outfits covering all the way up to your neckline like granny Goo Goo." She pursed her lips while staring over at Naydean. "Can I get an Amen?" She began clapping her hands together.

"Granny Goo, Goo." Her hand covered her mouth, shocked by Kennedy's comment. "Just because I don't show off my cleavage and butt crack doesn't mean I'm not sexy. I like to leave some things to the imagination."

The others tried hard to hold in their laughter from Kennedy's statements, knowing it was true. The Queen of England showed more skin than Naydean.

Flo was glad that Kennedy, being the outspoken one, said it first. Her friend needed to make a drastic change in the way she dressed. Naydean was thirty-three years old and never been married or had kids. Her wardrobe may be the reason for her solitude.

"Okay, let's get back to the business at hand." Flo stopped the insults before things went too far. "I've purchased your plane tickets, so just pay me back. I wanted us to be sitting next to each other."

Louisa had to be the realistic one who snapped her back to reality. "What does William think about your trip to the Magic

City?" Her brows lifted while waiting for an answer.

"In order for William to take me seriously, I have to show him how sincere I am about a career in fashion." She looked at her friend, hoping this told her what she wanted to know.

"Flo, do you think it is wise for you to do this? All I'm saying is that you and William have been together since teenagers. And I know he loves you and will give his life for you and those kids," Louisa stated, eyeing her from across the table.

"I know what I'm doing. William's mom knows and has agreed to keep the kids while I'm gone."

"Well, on that note, let's do it up right in "The Big M,"' Kennedy jumped from her seat, swinging her hips to an imaginary beat.

"Seeing that everyone is on board, I declare this meeting is adjourned. Now get out of my house eating up all my food."

Amid, the joking and laughter, Louisa's eyes communicated that she had some reservations about Flo leaving William in the dark about her plans.

Chapter 6

Sunday morning praise filled the air at Gomer Community Baptist Church. Flo and her husband sat in their usual seats on the fourth row. She felt inspired and ready to begin a new chapter in her life. Pastor Cephas always had a knack for simplifying God's Word that even a child could understand. Today, she sought clarity and guidance for the big leap she was about to take.

Her babies were in children church and the teens in young adult ministry, which meant she could enjoy the service without interruption. William looked handsome as always when he wore a suit and tie, but was still in the doghouse. He sat enjoying the angelic singers with a smile on his rugged face, but come two days from now, that smile would be wiped away when he realized that she had left for Miami.

She did her usual grocery shopping the previous day to ensure that the teens and William had plenty to eat while she was away. Her mother-in-law had the extra bedroom all set for her babies. Isabella always believed and supported her. She was overjoyed to learn that Flo had finally gotten the courage to leave her nest, spread her wings and soar. She would have asked her mother, but she wasn't in the best of health to handle two rambunctious kids. Come Tuesday, after everyone had left for school and work, she would call her friends to pick her up in the van they had rented and make her escape. Later, when they check into their rooms, she would call William, letting him know where she was and that she was safe. Flo knew that he would be upset but he'd get over it.

William reached for her hand and clasped it between his. His sudden gesture caused her to flinch. She wanted to pull away, still angry from his hurtful words, but she didn't. If it wasn't for the prying eyes of those man-hungry-women, looking for any signs of trouble in her marriage, she would have snatched her hand away.

The music ended, signaling it was time for Pastor Cephas to take his text. Flo prayed inwardly, hoping that God would give her a sign that she was making the right decision to go to Miami. Her heart and mind was made up and didn't want anything or anyone to change it.

"Good Morning church," Pastor Cephas shouted, rocking back and forth on his heels. He looked out into the crowd, wearing a huge smile on his face.

The congregation stood. It was apparent that the spirit of God was in the building. The soul-stirring songs from the choir earlier set the atmosphere for God to have His way.

He spoke with authority and eloquence when he asked, "Church, please turn your Bibles to Hebrews chapter eleven verse one."

Pages could be heard turning throughout the medium-sized church, where everybody knew everyone.

Once the sound of pages stopped, he continued, "Our text today is: Now faith is..."

Amen and hallelujahs roared through the room and she made sure that hers was heard among them. Flo freed her hand from William's and raised them toward heaven, thanking God for the subject He had given the pastor.

"I'm reading from the King James Version which reads, "Now faith is the substance of things hoped for, the evidence of things not seen.""

Flo's eyes lit up. She couldn't believe that Pastor Cephas' scripture reading was the same she'd been meditating on and reading all week. The Lord knew she needed faith to help her see spiritually the dream job she'd been hoping for. After the clapping and amen quietened down, she gave the pastor her undivided attention. Quickly, she pulled out a small tablet from her Bible protective case and began taking notes. She'd noticed William side-eying her, no doubt wondering what she was doing. He knew she only took notes in church when the message mirrored what was going on in her life.

He whispered, "Babe, you alright?" He put his arms around her.

Flo shook her head, signaling, no, and wondered how he could be so guileless. She believed her husband lived in his own world, oblivious to the one around him.

I want to tell him that he's the problem. I'm unhappy because of you and your lack of support, she thought.

Pastor Cephas continued, "For those of you who God is speaking to start your own business, write a book, or whatever He is directing you to do, don't let anyone talk you out of it. It is God who gives the vision. We are to have faith that He is able to bring it to pass. There are going to be many nights and days when you're going to have to stand in faith by yourself. God anointed you. Go chase after your dreams, even if it means you have to do it alone. The reason people around you don't understand your vision is that God didn't give it to them. He gave it to you. Most times, even those in your own home will try to discourage and talk you down from what God has gifted you to do."

Warm liquid spilled down Flo's face, causing William's hand to tighten around her shoulders. His act of endearment told her the pastor's word resonated with him. She never understood how her husband could sit under the word and it does not register in his heart to step out on faith and trust God.

With his arms still around her shoulders, he pulled her into him. She wanted to become vulnerable in his arms, but he was the problem and she was angry because he couldn't see it.

Pastor continued preaching his uplifting sermon. One that she really needed to hear, it was in God's plan for her to be chosen as one of the top five finalists. She'd tried telling William, but her words went into one ear and out the other. She even tried leaving the acceptance letter on the dresser, where he had to pass each day, but he never picked it up to read it.

If it wasn't for them being in church, surrounded by nosy people, she would ball her eyes out. How dare he clap his hands and amen everything the pastor preached and knew he wasn't going to do any of it?

Flo pulled some tissue from her purse and dried her eyes, as the pastor's message continued to fuel her soul. God had the final say when it came to the gift He'd blessed her with. William could either jump on board or get left behind.

If it wasn't for them being in church,

Flo wasn't her jovial self after church that day. It was mind-blowing how she'd heard a power pack message and yet, as soon as she left the church, allowed Satan to steal it. With all that she'd heard, she still craved for her family's support. She decided to skip their usual Sunday dining out and went home, pretending to be ill. Instead of ruining everyone's day, she told William to take the kids and that she would eat something later at home.

William kissed her on the lips, which was his way of comforting her. Too bad he lacked the ability to sense the hurt she was feeling on the inside.

"Go lie down, sweetie. And when I get back, I will come and check in on you."

She wanted to pull away but she didn't. No matter how she felt in that moment, he was still a good man and her husband. As a child, William grew up seeing his father taking care of his family, while his mother was a stay-at-home mom. If he had his way, that was what he wanted for her. He never pressed the issue because she worked close to home.

With her face pressed against his shirt, Flo held him close, praying that God would open his eyes to the truth. "I will," she muffled in his chest when what she wanted to do was pound against it with her fist, hoping to knock some sense into him, but she let him go and watched him and the kids drove off to eat Sunday dinner without her.

While walking into the kitchen to take something for her persistent headache, the ringing of her cellphone snapped her out of her dismal mood. "Hello," she answered above a whisper.

"How is my girl doing?" her mother asked.

"I'm fine," she hesitated, "I guess." Her heart felt as if it had broken into a million pieces when she heard her mother's voice. She wanted to fall into her arms like she had done as a child and ball her eyes out.

"You guess?" she questioned, concern lingering in her voice. "I just hung up with William. He said you weren't feeling well."

"I'm not physically ill, mother. My feelings are just hurt." She choked back the tears because they weren't going to change anything.

"Child, are you still moping around because he called your vision a pipedream?"

"And I'm not supposed to?" Her eyes widened in surprise to her mother's comment.

"You have received your answer from God, baby. It's his job to work on William's heart, not you. You just go and follow God's plan for your life. He gave you the vision to pursue a career in fashion, not William. You must realize that. When God gives you something, not everyone is going to see it. And that also includes your husband."

"But it hurts mama," she whimpered, like a wounded animal. "I want him to see it now."

"It doesn't work that way, child. William is not going to see it until God reveals it to him."

Her eyes walled in her head as she took two aspirin to stop the pounding in her head. "If he loves me, then he should see it."

"Look, I'm not going to argue with you about God's timing. But that is how life works. William is a good husband and father and he adores you."

"I know mama."

"I was married to your father for over thirty-five years before he passed. I know from experience that men don't always catch on quick when it comes to women and our feelings. That's why you have to show him and going on that trip will do just that."

"I hear you, but I wish that it didn't have to come to this."

"Baby, when a man thinks that he's going to lose his better half, he will move mountains to make sure that she is happy. It won't take long for reality to settle in. I promise, Flo, he will come around."

"I love you mama and thanks. You always have a way of making me feel better."

"That's my job. Now you go and take care of your last-minute details before leaving on Tuesday and watch this man travel to the end of the earth to be with you."

Chapter 7

Frustration occupied Flo's mind as unshed tears remained locked inside. Watching day turn into night, Flo remained hidden inside her bedroom. William and the kids returned home late that evening after visiting with his family. Every light was off throughout the house, including her bedroom. Thankfully, she'd closed the door because she'd overheard William telling the kids "not to disturb mommy."

Since everyone gave her the alone time she needed, Flo did something she hadn't done in weeks; watch a movie in its entirety. She fluffed her pillows behind her head and selected a movie from MovieFlix. She needed something funny to lift her spirits, so she stayed away from anything sad and emotional and chose BAPS, of all movies. In the twenty-something years of the movie existence, she never had any interest or desire to watch it. It seemed brainless, and besides, she didn't want to see her favorite actress, Halle Berry, playing unwitting. But, tonight, a good laugh was on the menu.

As soon as she made herself comfortable, the bedroom door opened. William, clothed in his pajamas stepped inside, crawling in next to her. The last thing she wanted was for him to touch her. His hands were a lethal weapon when it came to pleasure. She lay there, stiff as a board with her eyes focused on the television screen.

Then suddenly, he opened his mouth to speak.

"Flo, I know you're avoiding me." He rose to look over her shoulders.

Still, she didn't move.

"Baby, what's wrong? You've been quiet since we left church today."

She hunched her shoulders and said drily, "Nothing."

"Well, nothing sure does seem like something." His soft lips brushed against the base of her neck, making her want to surrender in his arms.

The only sound in the room came from the television, which he'd made her miss the introduction to the movie. Closed like a volt, her lips were sealed. Why hash up the same old conversation, knowing his response? If she heard him say 'pipedream' or 'midlife-crisis' one more time, she just might kick him where it hurts. It bothered her that he refused to hear her out and take her serious.

"So, you're just going to lie there and say nothing?"

"I'm tired and want to relax and watch this movie."

On a serious note, she could have cared less about the movie. She just didn't want to discuss her feelings with him. Her mind was made up about going to Miami and William could keep his opinions to himself.

"Isn't that the movie you said was stupid years ago and that you would never watch it?" he stated, pressing up against her.

"I'm allowed to change my mind." She tried shrugging his hand from her shoulders. He just couldn't take a hint. The next thing she knew, he grabbed her, flipping her body around to face him. She had to admit, William was one strong man. His action caught her by surprise. No one ignores him, not even his own wife. "William," she shouted. "What are you doing?"

"Woman, I don't have time for these games you're playing." He pulled her close to him, making sure she couldn't move. "Now, what is wrong with you?"

She swallowed hard and lied, "Nothing. I just want to lie here and enjoy this movie. Now can you release me? Please." Flo could tell by the look in his eyes that he didn't buy her excuse, but he complied with her wishes.

She turned back, facing the television as he held her close from behind.

The stress of having to keep her plans a secret from him was taking its toll on her. To keep from crumbling in front of him, she focused on the movie. Surprisingly, William didn't fall asleep. Underneath his breath, he laughed at the characters, Nisi and Mickey's antics. She had to admit that she was enjoying it as well. Flo never knew the storyline was about two young women who were growing tired of the lives they were living and wanted more. Unsatisfied with their jobs, they dreamt of opening a restaurant/beauty salon. They thought if they go to Los Angeles, California, to a casting call for the Heavy D video, that they could win the ten thousand dollars to seal the deal of becoming entrepreneurs.

Astonished by the storyline, Flo found herself sitting up in bed, propping her pillow against the backboard. It was as if they were describing her life, except for the ghetto fabulous scenes and occupations. She could have knocked herself against the head for never watching the movie. When she saw the trailer of her favorite actress wearing a gold tooth, it deterred her from going to see it at the theater. The movie seemed too stereotyped for her.

77

When she sat up, William moved in, laying his head on her lap. He couldn't see that what the characters in the movie wanted out of life was the same she expressed to him. Having the chance for hundreds of people and designers to see her work was a big deal. Getting her husband to see the importance of it was slim to none.

The movie did help to take her mind off her problems until Nisi's boyfriend, Ali said, "He was tired of hearing about all her pipedreams."

OMG!

William's body flinched at his words. Maybe he realized that he had used the same terminology when it came to her expressing her future plans to him. His hand rubbed against her covered legs. Now she knew that the character's words resonated with him.

Later, as the credits rolled, Flo was happy that she chose to watch "BAPS." As corny as it was, it made sense. She'd learned through the brainless comedy to never allow anyone to stop her from doing what she loved. Even if the person lying next to her couldn't see it, what matters was that she could. Hopefully, the ending of the movie would be hers, where Ali finally took his woman seriously. She prayed that William would do the same. No doubt, this movie was meant for her to see it at this appointed time. Twenty years ago, it wouldn't have had the same impact on her as it had now. Just like Nisi left town for Ali to take her serious, she planned to give William the same wake-up call.

Time passed quickly. It was ten at night. She grabbed the television remote from off the table near the bed and turned it off. William pulled her down next to him and held her in his arms. Without warning, the tears she'd been holding inside the entire day, spilled onto the mattress.

William heard the silent whimpers coming from his wife, knowing they were because of him. He wasn't the most sensitive man, but he loved his wife and wanted nothing but the best for her. He wanted to support her but was afraid that if she became successful and famous, she would leave him. Flo was always the one who went after whatever her heart and mind set out to do, but he was the one who played it safe. The fear of failure kept his dreams hostage. It kept him stuck and unwilling to venture out into the unknown. With his wife, it didn't matter if things didn't work out the first time. She would get back up and try again. He lacked that strength, and it showed in how he refused to support her.

Over the years, she'd tried convincing him to start his own business, but he'd always had an excuse as to why it was never the right time. Truth-be-told, he didn't have the courage or the faith to do so.

Instead of urging his wife to go after what she wanted, William tried silencing her words by making lite of them. As the love of his life lay balling her eyes out in his arms, he did nothing to console her. He lay there, pretending to be asleep. His family was his life and all he could think about was her seeing him as some dumb, country hick, especially when she start being exposed to men more polished than he.

Now he wanted to cry. He'd almost lost her to another man years ago. If it meant trying to stop her from going to Miami, then he'd do what he had to do to keep from losing her. The thought of them not being together frightened him.

The movie had hit home. He was the culprit, trying to snuff out his wife's dreams. He was Ali. He flinched when Ali's woman wanted to go chasing after her dreams. Instead of supporting her, the same as he did with Flo, he called her ideas a pipedream. In his heart, he prayed that things would work out for him and Flo as they had for the fictional characters.

William had doubts about opening up to her and sharing his fears because he was supposed to be her protector and provider. How would she view him if she knew that her husband was afraid of failing? He worked hard for what he had and didn't want to hit rock bottom if he put their life savings into a business that may or may not succeed. In another year, they would have not one, but two kids in college. How was he going to tell their babies that they couldn't attend school because he put everything he had in a sinking business?

He prayed that God would show him what to do. No one in his family had ever owned a business or gone to college. He was the foreman at his job. Instead of moving his family to the city, he chose to take a job in construction in town, which he drove an hour both ways. His position afforded them to live on the beautiful side of Gomer, Louisiana.

As much as he tried, he just couldn't talk her out from participating in that contest. He couldn't understand why she was so unhappy with the life she had. Why did she want to travel hundreds of miles away on a chance?

The movie did little to change his mind about how he felt about his wife's sudden fantasy of wanting to be in the spotlight. If that world rejected her, then what would she do?

In his heart, William knew that Flo wasn't the type of woman who was led by an impulse. She'd always put her family first, no matter what. When her father was on his deathbed, she stopped sewing to help her mother take care of him. Now, she was ready to go after what was hers. This time, he knew that she was serious and more driven than ever.

Thankfully, Flo had fallen asleep. He didn't know how much longer he could lie there, hearing her silent cries. He wanted to scoop her up into his arms and ease her pain. But how could he when he was responsible for it. He buried his head against her back, feeling ashamed of the man he had become.

Chapter 8

The walls were closing in on Flo as she tried to work in her shop. Since she wasn't accomplishing much, she decided to close early and knew just where to go to lift her spirits and hear some juicy gossip in the process. Her friends' beauty salon not only provided some of the best hairstyles in town, but it was filled with laughter and good times. The female patrons would air out their dirty laundry making her life not seem so bad. There were some things that a girl couldn't discuss with her husband, especially if the topic was about him.

Being the type of person who had to have things organized and put back into its perspective place, she cleaned up her shop before leaving. If only her home could be this tidy. Her babies kept their toys thrown all over the house. The oldest had clothes sprawled over the floors in their bedrooms. William would leave his smelly work boots by the living room door if she didn't stay on him about it.

After putting her sewing equipment away, Flo locked up, set the alarm before heading to the salon. She felt that it was a waste of time doing so because Gomer was a peaceful town. It was the type of place where people came to get away from the craziness of city life and raise a family. It made one appreciate and enjoy the simple things in life. Still, William insisted that she set the alarm, stating it wasn't a good idea to let down her guard. People from the surrounding cities did travel through Gomer, and that concerned him for her and his family safety. Everyone in their small town knew each other, but everyone else was outsiders and could be a potential predator.

Later, when she stepped inside Magic Fingers Salon, all her worries vanished in the air. She yelled, "Hey girls." There was something about them coming together. It took them back to their teen years when life consisted of nothing but parties, football games, and boys. She dropped her purse in one of the vacant chairs, heading over to where her friends were.

"My. My. My, look what the wind blew in," Kennedy joked while combing through a customer's hair.

It wasn't just any customer. It was Felicia Carmichael. The girl William dumped to be with Flo back in high school. As usual, she was dressed in a skinned-tight outfit, resembling a cougar on the prowl. Her painted nails were long and pointed like fangs ready to claw into its prey. Felicia's sewed-in hair reached down the middle of her back, which Flo had to admit, Kennedy could make even a stray cat look good.

"Don't act so surprised. It's not like I never come to visit," Flo quipped, adding a little sass in her tone and sway to her hips, knowing Felicia was eyeing her every move.

Felicia sat quietly in her seat, sizing Flo up from head to toe. Thankfully, she put on a sexy spring outfit. Her mother always taught her to never leave home looking disheveled. It has been years since they'd graduated high school and Felicia was still bitter over losing William to her.

"Uh-hh, if my math skills are correct," Louisa interrupted, sweeping hair off the floor. "It's been at least a month. Just because you have that new sew-in I did for you, don't mean that you have to stop coming to get your hair washed and cared for, missy."

"I know, that's right," Kennedy hollered, pointing over at her with a brush in her hand.

They laughed. Felicia faked a weak smile, knowing she was the last person Flo wanted to carry on a conversation with.

"Your natural hair can still fall out if it's not cared for properly. I hope you realize that" Naydean added, resting in a vacant chair after her customer left. "From over here, it seems to be holding up quite well."

"It better. I paid a lot of money for this hair and for Louisa to put it in." Flo tossed her hair from side to side. Felicia cut her eyes over at her. She didn't care because she still had the prize, for now. After William learned of her betrayal, she may lose him.

Flo took a seat next to Naydean, as Louisa, now busied herself restocking her area. Kennedy and Felicia discussed the latest gossip in Gomer, which she couldn't help but listen to. The more Kennedy worked her magic fingers through Felicia's head, the more gossip spilled from her lips. Her stories sounded like something straight out of a movie. One could not make up the things coming out of her mouth. Although she wasn't one of Flo's favorite people, listening to her stories was better than watching television. Besides, Felicia was a woman who got around.

"Girl, you heard about old man Peterson and his wife, Chloe?" Felicia asked, knowing they were waiting impatiently for her to spill the tea.

"No, what about them?" Kennedy asked, pulling out a flat iron to straighten Felicia's long mane.

Their ears were opened and eyes focused on her cosmetically injected ruby red lips as she dished the dirt.

"Well... I heard that the cane he uses to help him walk is just a prop." She smacked her lips, looking around at them.

"What...girl, that man is crippled. God is going to strike you down for talking bad about the handicap," Naydean reprimanded Felicia for spreading such lies. She turned in her chair, opened the drawer near her, pulled out a Bible, and waved it at her.

Kennedy stopped styling Felicia's hair and responded, "Stop being so serious, girl. Lighten up and have a little fun," she scolded Naydean with her eyes. "Now, what were you saying, Felicia, about Mr. Peterson's cane?"

Louisa turned from stocking and spat, "I know one thing, you better not come to Florida with all that foolishness. Or we're going to leave your boring behind in Gomer."

"Boring?" Naydean shouted. Her eyes widened as if surprised that she wasn't the life of the party.

"Let's get back to the story," Kennedy said. "A prop for what?"

Flo was glad Kennedy butted in. She wanted to know what happened, even if it was from her nemesis.

Felicia continued, "A friend saw him last week, sneaking into Mrs. Johnson's back door."

"Hold up," Kennedy paused, resting a hand on Felicia's shoulders. "Mrs. Johnson, the undertaker's wife?"

"The one and only," she said with her head bobbing up and down. "I heard when he got out of his car, he looked around. I guess to see if anyone was watching and tossed his cane in the backseat of the car. Then, he headed to the back of Mrs. Johnson's house."

"That could have been anyone," Naydean remarked, folding her arms like an old woman.

"True, but when he exited the home two hours later, Mr. Johnson was out back waiting for him with his pistol. It was said that he ran in a panic and passed his own car. Whatever limp he had, straightened up when he was staring into the barrel of Mr. Johnson's gun."

The ladies laughed so hard, even Naydean had to join in. They didn't hear the bell alerting them that a customer had entered the shop.

Louisa directed the customer to the shampoo bowl. "What's so funny?" she asked, leaning back to get her hair washed.

But they couldn't speak. They were in tears, laughing at Felicia's story.

"Girl, I can't believe his old behind had the nerve to be in an undertaker's house," Kennedy screamed with laughter. Everyone knows that if you look like you're on the brink of death, Mr. Johnson is at your front door."

"If Mr. Peterson hadn't ran as fast as he did, he would have been embalmed right there on the spot and ready for burial." That was the reason Flo loved coming to her friends' shop, someone always had a great story to tell.

Louisa changed the subject, now getting up in Flo's business. "Flo, have you told William that you will be leaving Wednesday, instead of Tuesday?"

Felicia's head snapped in Flo's direction at the mention of William's name. "Where are you going?" Felicia asked with a cheeky smile.

"I don't care to share." Flo turned in the swivel chair, giving Louisa the evil eye. "No." She really didn't want to discuss her business in front of Felicia.

The others now turned their eyes on Flo as well, putting her on the spot. They knew her history with Felicia. Why were they so eager to discuss her and William's business in front of her?

"Girl, don't go ruining your marriage by keeping secrets from your man," Louisa advised as she leathered her customer's head with shampoo.

"I have everything under control, thank you, so don't go worrying about me," Flo lied, knowing she and William were at odds with each other. "The three of you just better have your bags packed." She faked a smile, but inside, she was sweating bullets. The bold decision she was making to go to Florida could either make or break her marriage.

"Well, as long as you know what you're doing." Louisa winked, giving her a weak smile as she towel-dried her customer's hair.

"I have to agree, Flo," Naydean added, tugging at her skirt that nearly touched the floor. "You guys have been together since high school. A love like yours only comes around once. Please don't mess it up."

Felicia scrunched up her nose at Naydean's comment.

"Look, I know you all are concerned about me—"

Kennedy interrupted, "William will be alright. He's a big boy. I don't need you two trying to discourage Flo from going to Miami. Heck, I've been looking forward to it because I'm single and ready to mingle." Felicia slapped her, a high five as they cackled.

"Anyway, thanks for the advice, but I have to do what I have to do. There is no turning back now."

"Okay, I'm just saying. You know how all those old, lonely, desperate church women been eyeing William over the years. They will be happy knowing you're out of the picture so that they can get their wrinkled old hands on him," Louisa laughed.

Felicia smacked her lips with a moan, knowing she was one of them. It would be over her dead body before she got her claws into her husband.

Louisa's comment made Flo's blood boil. "I wish they would try. I will be upside their heads so fast they wouldn't know what hit them." She leaned back into her seat, looking over in Felicia's direction. Flo was no fool. She did take heed to Louisa's words.

"Go do you. If William leaves you because of this, then he wasn't the man you thought he was in the first place. And you two need to stop being the grim weepers," Kennedy stated.

Louisa and Naydean shot Kennedy a nasty look.

"This woman is excellent at what she does. We all love wearing her designs. The people that have the power to get her designs into the public eyes is never going to see them if she only sells them in Gomer." Kennedy stopped flat-ironing Felicia's hair and pointed it at Flo as she was talking. "God didn't give you the gift to sew just for this place. Your designs can put some of those in Hollywood, New York, and Paris to shame."

"Thank you, Kennedy," she smiled, feeling like she could take on the world by her friend's powerful words. "I needed that."

"We are not trying to talk you out of going, Flo. But you have a family. You have responsibilities. We have been best friends since forever. I would be devastated if anything happens to you and William. You know I want you to win and go out there and show these fancy designers what rural America has to offer," Louisa declared as she put her customer under the hair dryer.

Naydean sat quietly. Her head bouncing back and forward like a ball in tennis match, agreeing with everyone.

"I'm thankful to have great friends like you all. William and I will be okay. I trust and believe that God's hands are in the midst of this."

Chapter 9

Tired from a hard day's work, William dragged himself to go inside the grocery store to purchase items his wife had forgotten the previous day. Normally, she was pretty thorough, following her list to the letter. As much as he hated going, he'd do anything to please her.

He raced from one aisle to the next, trying to get in and out as quickly as possible. Today, he was in no mood for shooting the breeze with anyone. Gomer was a town where no one could go unnoticed. With his shopping cart in speed mode, he propelled through the store like lightning. Then, as luck would have it, he'd almost crashed into the woman he dated briefly back in high school. With force, he pulled back hard, stopping it within inches of her.

"Are you blind?" she screamed, trying to protect her designer shoes more than herself.

She never looked up at him until he said, "I'm sorry, Felicia. I wasn't watching where I was going."

Like a puppet being pulled by its string master, her head shot up and a flirtatious smile formed on her plump lips. "William, I didn't know it was you." Her entire body moved as she spoke.

William couldn't lie and he wasn't blind. Felicia was a beautiful woman, but she was shallow. Everything had to revolve around her. He swore he had never met a more selfish person. He tried pushing his shopping cart around her to make his exit, only it wasn't that easy. She pressed her hand on the cart to stop him from leaving.

"What's your rush, Will-ll?"

She tried seducing him with her eyes.

He rolled his eyes in his head, hating the way she sang his name. "I don't have time,

Felicia. I have to get home to my, WIFE." He emphasized.

"She's not at home," she mentioned, toying with her necklace while undressing him with her eyes.

"How do you know where my wife is?" he demanded.

"She is at Magic Fingers Salon with those friends of hers. You must be so proud of her?" Her voice sounded low and soft, trying to tempt him.

Something told him to push pass her and leave but curiosity got the better of him. "You don't even care for my wife, so what's the excitement in your voice about?"

"Oh, Will-ll, don't be that way. We are all adults now." She moved in closer to him, making him uncomfortable and hoping none of the nosey town folks spotted her trying to push up on him. The people in their community loved his wife and wouldn't hesitate to spill the beans on him.

"Right," he yelped.

"She was just boasting about her winning a top spot in some fashion competition in Miami."

He didn't want to hear any more of Felicia's blah blah blah. He tried to leave again but now, she stood inches from him. Things haven't changed over the years. She still thought that she had a chance. One thing he'd never done was cheated on his wife. He loved her more than life and would never bring that type of drama onto their doorsteps.

He took a couple steps back to put some space between them. "What do you want? We are not in high school anymore."

"I just want you to know if things don't work out between you and Flo, I'm always here." Her hand touched the opening of her blouse and then glanced back up at him.

Before William could respond, Mrs. Jenkins, one of his mother's gossipy neighbors, came strolling down their aisle. Now he had reasons to sweat. The old lady could have been a news reporter. His heart pulsated as she moved like a snail in their direction.

"William? Son...what are you doing standing here with her?" One of Mrs. Jenkins eyes glanced over in Felicia's direction, giving her the stink nose.

"Good evening, Mrs. Jenkins." Invisible sweat rushed down his face. He tried faking a smile like he was happy to see her, but the way she was grilling them over with her eyes made it hard. "I would give you a big hug, but I just left work. I'm here picking some items for my wife," he felt the need to add.

"It don't matter, baby. I'm an old lady. I'm not trying to catch no man." She turned, ripping Felicia into pieces with her good eye.

William leaned in, giving her one of those church hugs. Filled with lust, Felicia stood, watching his behind. Now he knew he had to get out of there and fast. If he wasn't married, she would never be the type of woman he would join in holy matrimony with, no matter how gorgeous she was.

Mrs. Jenkins caught him by surprise. She looped her arms through his, leaving Felicia on aisle nine speechless and looking played.

"Baby, you looked like you needed some rescuing?" Mrs. Jenkins asked, smiling up at him.

"Thank you, Mrs. Jenkins. You are a lifesaver. I can't understand why she doesn't give up?"

"I'll tell you why son. Nobody had a gun pointed to your head making you stand there and talk to her. You had every opportunity to leave."

"But—"

"I'm not finished," she scolded. "You chose to stay there and entertain her foolishness. That's why women like her believe that they have a chance. It gives them hope when you don't walk away."

Feeling like a child with the need to defend himself, he said, "I told her that I didn't have time to talk."

"Well, you didn't try hard enough to leave. That woman has a bad reputation around town as being a home wrecker. You don't want to invite that type of trouble into your home."

"I hear you, Mrs. Jenkins. And thanks for the advice."

They paid for their groceries and William helped her load her bags into her car.

"Now, you get on home to that beautiful wife and those adorable kids. Don't let the devil come in and steal what God has blessed you with. You hear me?"

"Yes, ma'am."

He waved her goodbye and headed to his truck. As he closed his door, Felicia came swaying her hips out the grocery store. He revved up the engine and flew out that parking lot as if his life depended on it.

Mrs. Jenkins was right, but it haunted him that Flo was telling everyone about that competition. Frankly, he was tired hearing about it. He didn't want his wife chasing around the world when their paradise was right there in Gomer, Louisiana.

It infuriated William that his wife was being chummy with her enemy. Felicia used every opportunity to come on to him. It wasn't as if Flo didn't know it. Today proved that she hadn't changed.

An hour later, William found his wife wrapped in a towel in their bedroom. "Hey babe," he greeted, kissing her on the lips. He kept the distance between them because he still wore his work clothes.

She pinched her nose with her hand and said, "How was your day?"

"It was okay." He began to undress, heading to the shower.

She followed him inside the bathroom. "Just okay? What happened?"

He really didn't feel like talking. While driving home, he had a list of things he wanted to discuss with her. He'd forgotten what he wanted to say when he saw her standing there wrapped in a towel, looking sexy as ever. Mrs. Jenkins was right. He was blessed and most times, too stupid to appreciate it.

"Nothing happened, Flo. I'm working in these hot elements every day. It's just exhausting some days."

"If you owned your own business, you wouldn't come home worn out like this."

"We're not going to discuss that tonight, baby." The last thing he wanted was for her to make him feel worse. He wanted his wife tonight and didn't want to hear all that foolish talk about something that wasn't going to happen.

After his shower, he found her asleep across the bed. He knew she couldn't be tired because according to Felicia, she spent her day at the beauty salon telling the town her business. He'd tried his best to save her from the embarrassment later on, but she was bent on this fashion kick.

"Flo. Baby," he whispered, trying to wake her up. "Wake up and get under the cover."

She yawned and stretched, asking, "What time is it?"

"It's only seven-thirty."

The soft, sexy smelling fragrance she wore drove him wild and she knew it was his favorite. As she climbed into her side of the bed, he followed, hoping he'd get lucky tonight. To his surprise, it wasn't happening. Before her head hit the pillow, she was out like a light. He mashed his head against the pillow with the feeling that he was losing his wife. Lately, they had become distant. He knew it was because of him. Frustrated, he returned to his side of the bed and prayed that sleep would come and take him out of his misery.

Chapter 10

It was Tuesday morning, one more day before she made her departure for a chance of a lifetime. Her five-year-old twins were being little terrors, harassing the older twins by hiding their personal belongings. Little did they know, come tomorrow night, they would be staying with their grandmother until she returned from Miami, hopefully, a winner.

"Landon. London," she yelled, stopping them dead in their tracks. "What are the two of you up to?"

"We're not doing nothing," they said in unison, trying to sound innocent when she knew they weren't.

"Leave your brother and sister alone and come eat your breakfast."

"We coming mommy."

It took them a little too long, so Flo decided to investigate. They must think she was born yesterday. Flo tiptoed down the hallway to the living room entrance. They were snickering while going through William Jr.'s cellphone. The only thing she could do was shake her head. Never once as a child could she remember annoying her older brother. Or maybe she just blotted it out.

They were so young but yet, like two little women, discussing what they were seeing in Jr.'s phone. She wasn't ready to reveal herself, she watched, taking in more of their conversation.

"Brother, girlfriend has a big ole head, London."

"Mm-hmm, sure do," London agreed, pursing her lips. They both sat with their legs crossed as they continued strolling through his phone.

They burst into laughter. She had to admit, they were funny and adorable.

"Looks like something wrong with her eye though," London said, putting her face closer to the screen.

"Ooooooooooooo," they sang in unison.

Landon placed her hands over her eyes and screamed, while London held on to the phone. "He got his mouth all over that bighead girl."

"Yuck! That's nasty," London squealed. "Our bother gonna catch an eye disease kissing that girl."

Flo covered her mouth to keep them from hearing her laughing at the door. Although they were wrong taking their brother's phone, she had to admit, they were two of the funniest kids.

"Mama," William Jr. yelled, snapping her back to the reason why she went looking for the twins. "Those little monsters took my phone out my room."

She cleared her throat, alerting them that they had been busted. "Give me that phone and get your tales in the kitchen," she demanded, retrieving William Jr.'s phone.

Their eyes widened with fear as she towered over them.

"I have your phone Jr.," Flo yelled, marching the twins down the hallway. "And you and Julia need to come eat before you are late for school."

Flo set the table while she waited for the rest of her family to come take their seats. Her babies jumped into their chairs, grabbing their glasses of orange juice in front of them.

Still in a foul mood after not getting what he wanted from her last night, William walked into the dining room, dressed for work, looking delicious. He dropped into his seat with his head hung low. On the sly, she cut her eyes over in his direction, smiling inwardly. If only he knew how scrumptious he looked and what it did to her when he sulked. But she had to put her hormones in check. She wasn't caving in, no matter how tempting the temptation that sat in front of her was. He had to understand that spitting out hurtful words came with a hefty price. It didn't matter how handsome he looked from across the table. He couldn't seriously think that bringing her down would make her want to be intimate with him.

Julia finally graced them with her presence when she came prancing into the room all dolled up, wearing every designer labels, except hers. William's head snapped up from his brooding when he looked at her attire. "Where do you think you're wearing that outfit too?" he asked, his brows rose with parental concern.

"Dad-ddy," she whined, shocked by her father's disapproval. "All the girls wear tights to school. They are the replacements for pants."

"I don't care what other girls are wearing. I'm only concerned about you."

Without him saying another word, Julia left to go change into something more suitable. The tights were so tight that it showed every crease imaginable. She respected her father's opinion and did as he asked. At times, she could be a little rebellious, making William become more authoritative than usual.

The twins began giggling at their sister when she left the room. Landon, being the more outspoken one said, "She needed to go and take them booty pants off with her chicken legs."

London turned, watching her sister leave the room, and then turned and looked at Landon. "Uh-huh, she do got some bird legs. I hope ours don't look like that when we grow up."

They snickered amongst themselves.

Flo watched her five-year-old girls talking to each other like grown women. "Stop talking about your sister, girls," she said, placing their plates in front of them.

Jr. had to throw his two cents in with the twins. "They are telling the truth." He gulped down his glass of milk.

Before she could stop him, William cut in saying, "You heard your mama. Stop making fun of your sister."

The mute finally spoke. He had been sitting in silence ever since entering the room.

In her mind, she was the one who should have been mad. Tomorrow, she would be on a plane, heading to Miami. Instead of going with her soulmate, she would be traveling with her girlfriends.

Julia made her way back to the table dressed in a fashionable jumpsuit. Flo tried discussing and showing her new young teen collection to Julia, but she turned up her nose at the gesture. She understood that her daughter was at that age where she worried about what others thought more than being her own person. She hoped that fashion would bring them closer but instead it drove a wedge between them. Flo desired a closer relationship with her oldest daughter but, she was a daddy's girl.

"Daddy, is this better?" Julia asked, knowing her father didn't play when it came to her leaving the house looking like anything other than a decent young woman.

"Better, baby girl," he said, swallowing down a mouth-full of grits.

She smiled, joining them in breakfast.

113

The twins continued their antics while the others ate their breakfast in silence. No doubt, her older teens were aware that something was going on between her and their father from the way they kept staring at her and William. The kids were used to his playful, happy go lucky mood and this morning, he behaved like a big sourpuss.

Later, after the kids left for school, William hung back, alerting Flo that something was on his mind or he wanted what he didn't get from her last night. Trying not to notice his pacing back and forth in the kitchen, she continued to wash the dishes. Whatever it was eating at him, she wished he would just spit it out.

Then without warning, he said, "What was that about last night?" He walked over to the sink beside her, folding his arms while waiting for an answer.

She knew what he was talking about, but yet, she played naive. "Can you be more specific, William? I don't read minds." She stopped drying the plate and faced him. "You are the one in a foul mood this morning."

"I wouldn't be in a foul mood if you weren't pretending to be asleep last night."

"What?" Flo stared at her husband as if he was speaking a foreign language. "Pretending to be asleep," she snapped, trying her best not to go off on him about his inconsiderate attitude. "In case you haven't noticed, I have a job too."

"Sitting at a desk, sewing all day is hardly what I call work."

No, he didn't just belittle what I do, again?

"Now, you got your answer to why I went to sleep early last night. Just because I'm not out in the heat every day doesn't mean I don't work."

"You know what I meant, baby," he said, trying to smooth things over.

She distanced herself from him and said, "No, I don't know what you mean." Infuriated wasn't the word for what she was feeling at that moment. Her reactions were mixed with hurt bubbling over into anger. Her husband really didn't have a clue of how the words that escaped from his lips made her feel or if he really cared.

"Why have you been so cold toward me lately? I have done nothing but try to love you. And you have done nothing but reject my affection."

At first, she wanted to tell him that, come tomorrow, she would be on a plane, heading down south, but she held her tongue. He had no respect for the work she do. She bridled her tongue instead and said, "If you took the time to listen to the words that come out of your mouth concerning my work and being chosen to go to Miami, then you would know why I refused your affection."

"Woman, what are you talking about?" he asked, confusion written over his face.

She waved him off and left the kitchen. If she stayed in his presence, there was no telling what she might say or do. Violence wasn't in her DNA, but she wanted to knock some sense into that hard head of his.

To her surprise, he followed on her heels into the bedroom. He grabbed her by the arm, spinning her around to face him. "Flo, are you going through the change or something?"

With all her might, she tried to pull away from him, but he held her tight. "Change?" She continued to wiggle in his arms. "Just because I want to pursue a career that I've always dreamed of since a little girl doesn't mean that I'm going through something. Now let me go," she growled.

He released his hold on her. If her eyes were seeing correctly, a hint of sadness overshadowed his face. Without saying goodbye, he turned and left the room. Her chest rose and fell at the thought of what she'd just witnessed.

What is he so afraid of?

Still, inside the bedroom, Flo heard the front door slam and William sped off in his truck. Now, she was confused. What was

going on with her husband? She had no doubt
that he loved her.

Chapter 11

It was Wednesday, the day of her long-awaited trip. Excitement and sadness came over her as she walked through her bedroom. The last thing she wanted was to leave anything of importance behind. To keep William from getting suspicious, she had Louisa to stop by yesterday to retrieve her luggage and designs for the competition. After her family left for school and work, all she needed to do was pack her makeup and toiletries.

William was still in his foul mood, so she pretended to be asleep when he left this morning to keep from getting into another spat with him. The look in his eyes after their argument the previous day was that of an insecure man. What was he unsure about? Flo loved her husband with her entire heart. The last thing she wanted to do was jeopardize her

119

marriage. Ever since she brought up the subject of wanting to try this fashion thing again, he became argumentative. He began to talk down and discourage her from doing so. The William she'd been seeing the last month was not the man she fell in love with years ago. The young boy she married would have had her back, even if she failed. He would have been there to pick her up, dust her off, and tell her to try again.

When she finished packing her makeup bag, she pulled out a letter she had addressed to William. No doubt, when he comes home tonight and knew that she went against his wishes, he would be furious, but that was a chance she was willing to risk. There was no way she was going to look back over her life with any regrets. She had no power to make him follow his passion, but she wasn't going to allow him to stop her. She'd had doubts, missed many opportunities, and had no plans of missing another. If William loved her the way he claimed, then he'd understand why she had to do what she did.

William was a creature of habit, so she placed the letter on the dresser, near his cologne bottles. That was the one place she knew he would go after taking a long hot shower. One thing about her man; he loved smelling good, even if he had no place to go. She touched the letter for the last time and said a small prayer, hoping he would understand her decision.

A car horn sounded in the driveway. It was time for Flo to see what God had in store for her. Like the characters, Nisi and Mickey, she was chasing a dream and prayed it came true for her as well. Before letting go of the letter, she kissed it; placed it back on the dresser and left.

Minutes later, she hopped in the front seat of the van. A tug seemed to pull at her heartstring. Still, she couldn't shake the sorrow burning in his eyes when he tried discouraging her from going to Miami. If he wasn't dead-set against it, they could have made it a romantic getaway, free of charge.

But he allowed his pride to override his better judgment.

"What's wrong with you?" Kennedy asked. Her face twisted out of sort.

"Nothing," her voice sounded shallow as she closed the door.

"You're not having second thoughts, are you, Flo?" Louisa asked, glancing over at her from the driver's seat.

"Oh no," she snapped, turning to face everyone. "I hate leaving while William and I are not on speaking terms. I pray that he understands my decision." She stopped and gathered herself before the tear that was threatening to fall makes its entrance down her cheek.

Naydean sat in the back seat with Kennedy with a look that said, "I told you so," written over her cover girl, made-up face. Before she could open her mouth to voice her opinion on the matter, Louisa diverted it. "Girl, William loves you. He will eventually understand that this is your God-given purpose in life."

"I hope so because he shut me down each time I tried bringing the subject up." If it wasn't for his and her mother, encouraging her to go after what she wanted, Flo might have changed her mind. Women had put their careers on the back burner for men for years. Now, they were saying it was their time to come from behind the shadows of the suit and tie age and have careers of their own while raising a family. His mom had always wanted to be a nurse but believed her mother when she said, *"A woman's place was in the home, raising her children and taking care of their husband."* Therefore, his mom expressed that this was a new era for women to take charge of their lives and career paths.

Naydean unsnapped her seatbelt, scooting up behind Flo and said, "We got you, Flo. If it wasn't meant to be, God wouldn't have allowed you to be one of the five finalists."

Shocked by her positive words, they turned and looked at Naydean, giving her a winning smile. Flo needed to hear that. It was reassuring, especially coming from her. Naydean was raised by her grandmother and some of her views were outdated and set women back fifty years. Thankfully, she was slowly realizing that it was okay for a woman to have her own mind, thoughts, and feelings.

Kennedy stared at Naydean and asked, "Who are you and what have you done with Naydean, the bearer of bad news?"

They laughed as Flo gave them the green light to pull out of the driveway. It was now or never. "Let's do this, girls."

Instead of catching the airplane that Loran Sinclair had paid for, she and her friends decided to cash in their tickets, rented a luxury van to take a road trip in style. Needless to say, Flo was happy and scared at the same time. She was about to embark on a new chapter in her life and loved the surge of confidence it gave her once she accepted the fact that she deserved to live her life to its fullest.

William entered the front door to a noiseless and dark house. It wasn't like Flo and the kids not to be at home at this late hour of the day. He assumed that maybe she was running around town with the kids. Anyway, he pushed his concerns aside and headed straight to the bedroom. Today had been one of the hardest days in his construction career. One of his men fell several feet from a building. It was God's grace and mercy that he wasn't fatally injured. His safety belt broke his fall, but it took over an hour for firemen to lower him to safety.

Tired of being consumed with anger at his wife and her constant talking about some competition in Miami, he needed to feel her tender touch right about now. After what happened today, it put his life into perspective. Life was too short and the last thing he wanted to do was walk into his own home not speaking to the woman he loved. Flo was his rock, his good thing. No other woman could love him the way she did.

Desperate for a hot shower, he headed to the bathroom to freshen up before his wife returned home. He stepped inside and allowed the hot water to stream down his tired body, wishing his woman was in there with him. It was stressful being angry at her for no reason. When she returned home tonight, he had a lot of apologizing and making up to do.

Later, he dried off and headed to the dresser where he kept his collection of cologne. He knew the exact one to wear that drove his wife wild when she smelt it on him. He noticed a letter addressed to him in Flo's handwriting, propped against one of the bottles. For some reason, the letter made him nervous. His family was nowhere in sight, which wasn't like her. Now, his imagination began to take over, making him think the worse.

He knew that she was unhappy about him not supporting her. Now, he had to wonder if his lack of support and not taking her serious caused her to take the kids and leave him. Quickly, he snatched the letter from the dresser and allowed the edge of the bed to support the weight of his tensed body.

His hands shook like never before as he tried to read the letter. He thought that the near-death of a co-worker almost scared him out of his mind, but this was different, was he about to lose his wife and kids also? He took a deep breath, braced himself, and prepared for the worse.

Dear William,

I fell in love with you the first time I laid eyes on you. I never met a man that loved God and his family with all his heart and soul. You have made me the happiest woman in the world over the years, but lately, you have been dismissing God's calling on my life. I cannot understand why it's hard for you to support me and my dreams of becoming a professional designer.

Just in case you are wondering, Landon and London are at your mother's house. Jr. and Julia are out with their friends and will be home around eleven tonight. As for me,

I am headed to Miami. Don't worry, the girls are with me. I wanted us to go together, but you shut me down each time I tried discussing it with you.

His eyes stung from the tears that began to swell in his eyes. His wife had to get the support that he should have given her from others. Even his mother knew what was going on.

I must tell you that you hurt me to the core, knowing that you could have cared less about my dreams. I never expected you to hurt me with your words the way that you have over the last month.

William placed the letter on his lap. He couldn't control his emotions any longer. The thought of hurting his wife made him sick to his stomach. How cold-hearted could he have been? All Flo wanted was for him to take her serious and have faith in her, but he let his queen down, leaving her to find the strength to go after what she wanted alone.

He retrieved the letter, continuing where he left off.

God has blessed me with a chance of a lifetime. It hurt deeply when you didn't acknowledge the letter I placed on the dresser last month of me being chosen as one of the five finalists. I can't understand why you got so angry and distant when I tried to share my good news with you.

I'm sorry that I had to leave this way, but I'm not like you. I can't bottle up my dreams and store them away as if they never existed. I will not sit idle while the life is being sucked out of me, wondering what I could have become.

Don't ever believe that I'm tired of being with you. I'm dissatisfied of not having the career that I should have had years earlier. I will never regret marrying you and you giving me four beautiful children. But I'm losing myself while I'm catering to everyone else's wishes except mine.

I will call you once we arrive in Miami and I pray that this is not the end for us.

Love always,
Flo.

William tossed the letter aside and fell back onto the bed with his hands pressed upon his face, hating himself for allowing things to have gone this far. His ignoring and making little of her ideas didn't seem to stop her from leaving. The only thing that ran through his mind was; what if she loved it in Florida and didn't want to return home to him? Who was he, but a construction worker? William thought that Flo could have done a lot better than him and the idea of losing her terrified him.

Chapter 12

Upset with himself for missing the warning signs of Flo leaving, William dressed and headed to a sports bar on the outskirts of town. Since his mom had the kids and Flo was somewhere having the time of her life, he didn't want to be alone. He wasn't much of a drinker, but tonight, he had to have one. Nothing heavy, just something to numb the hurt he was feeling inside. The more he thought of Flo leaving without telling him, the angrier he became. In his mind, his beloved wife had betrayed his trust by keeping secrets from him. She told everyone where she was going except her husband. What kind of marriage did they have, if they didn't have trust?

Unable to see his faults in his wife departure, William decided to go and do what he wanted to do tonight. It was ten o'clock at night, and he hadn't so much as heard a peep from his wife. The marriage must not be as important to her if she didn't have the decency to call and tell him if she was okay.

William parked his vehicle in a well-lit area outside the sports bar, being careful to watch his surroundings. Once inside, he surveyed the room, hoping he wouldn't run into any busybodies. If he did, why should it matter? His wife left, leaving a letter behind because she did not have the courage to face him. The more William rehearsed the situation in his mind, the more he forgot that it was he who was at fault.

The bar seemed to be calling his name. At first, he decided to drink something light, but his foul mood made him want something stronger. He slid upon the stool where they had the channel on golf of all things.

Now, hating that he left home, he sat brooding over his wife's gutsy move to go after what she wanted. If only he had the same drive, maybe he could open a business. A bartender interrupted his internal whining.

"What can I get you to drink, sir?"

"I'll take a beer for starters," he stated as the dark-haired, twenty-something male cleaned a shot glass with a towel.

"For starters, huh?" the young man asked, staring at him with a smile. "That means you plan on being here for a while. Just make sure you have a driver to take you home. Or, I will have to stop serving you."

"I'm not planning on getting wasted." William stared up at the man, giving him a reassured half smile.

"Don't matter." He sat the glass he was cleaning in a rack, and then turned, giving William a matter-of-fact look. "Buzz driving impairs good judgment on the roads too."

"Just make it one beer and call it a wrap, okay," he snapped. He wasn't in the mood for any lectures tonight. Bitterness continued to consume him because of his wife's sneaky departure. Although he wasn't happy about her wanting to start a new career, he still deserved respect as a husband to know what she was up to. It angered him to know that she trusted her friends with her secrets than him.

The bartender placed a beer mug in front of him. He sat there for what seemed like hours, nursing his drink, although it had only been thirty or forty minutes. Why he ordered the alcoholic beverage was beyond him. It tasted disgusting. The first sip nearly made him gag. He just wanted the pain to stop. Unable to swallow any more of the drink, he pushed it aside and turned his attention to the television mounted on the wall. Sadly, even the sport channel couldn't cheer him up. He was down in the dumps and nothing seemed to lift his spirits. He needed his woman, but she was miles away, possibly surrounded by men more cultured than he. Who was he kidding? He was a country boy with no degrees behind his name.

William sat lamenting over not being good enough when a pair of hands touched him on the shoulders. It had to be a woman because no man would dare touch him that way. He spun his stool around to see who those soft hands belonged to. He should have known that it was Felicia. Who else would be that bold to walk upon a man she didn't know?

"William, you're the last person I expected to see this late at night."

Seductively, she moved her body closer, giving him an eye full of what she was working with.

He scrunched up his face. She was the last person he wanted to see. "Oh, it's you," was all he could say. *This woman doesn't take rejection well.* William knew that she still had a thing for him after all those years, which was why he'd better stay sober tonight. It was bad enough he was longing for his wife's touch. William sure didn't want his senses clouded by alcohol, causing him to make the worst decision of his life. Flo would never forgive him for sleeping with her enemy. Felicia never got over the fact that he dumped her to date,

Flo. Ever since that day, she had been trying to put a wedge between him and his wife.

With an attitude, she said, "Is that all you have to say, 'Oh it's you?'" Her neck rotated back and forth like a slinky toy.

She eased on a stool next to him. William called for the bartender to settle his tab. If he stayed there with Felicia any longer, people would talk. Most of the residents knew their history together. True, he was mad at his wife for leaving without telling him, but he would never sleep with another woman behind her back if he wanted to continue living.

"Aren't you here with someone?" he asked, giving her a hint to leave.

"Yes," she said, lowering her brows and licking her lips at him. "I'm here with you."

Before he could tell her off, the bartender reappeared and asked, "Can I get your lady friend something to drink?"

He couldn't get the words out fast enough. "She's not with me." William paid for his unfinished drink and prepared to leave.

"Will, are you going to let me drink alone?"

She brushed a hand full of weaved hair from her face, and then slightly eased up her skirt, exposing her thighs.

This woman just can't take a hint.

"Don't call me that. Go find your own man and drink with him." If he wasn't a gentleman, he would go off on her.

She grabbed his arm before he could walk off, "At least, my man didn't leave town without telling me." Wearing a smug look and smile on her face, Felicia knew she'd hit a nerve.

His eyes widened, wondering how she knew that his wife had left town. Now he was livid. "Well, I suggest you go where your imaginary man is and stop trying to push up on me because I will never want you," he stressed.

He left her sitting on the stool with her mouth wide open. William stormed out the bar door. He didn't know what to make out of Felicia's statement. His wife would never confide in someone like her, but then again, what did he know? She left town without as much as a goodbye, making him wonder if he really knew her at all.

Flo called home to let William know that she and the girls had arrived in Florida safely, but no answer. She hung up and tried his cellphone, the same; no answer. Worry began to overtake her; causing her to think the worse. The last thing she wanted to do was destroy her marriage. William always answered his cellphone, even if it was a telemarketer calling. She tried both phones one last time with no success.

Once she and the girls unpacked their things, before going out on the town, although it was late, she called her mother-in-law to check in on her babies.

The phone rang several times before her mother-in-law answered.

"Hello," a sleepy voice answered.

"It's me, Flo," she said, feeling down after not been able to reach her husband. "Sorry to wake you. Just called to tell you we made it to Miami."

"Oh, baby, I'm glad you called. I've been praying that you all make it down there safely."

"Thank God, there were no problems on the road."

"Flo...baby, what's with the sad voice?"

"Have you heard from William?"

"No, I thought, he would have called and checked on the kids. But, I haven't heard from him since yesterday."

"I'm scared. I left him a letter, letting him know that I would call him when I arrived here in Florida. But he hasn't answered the house or his cell phone."

"Baby, look, don't start second-guessing your decision. I'm William's mother and I know that this is God's will for your life. I know my son. He's somewhere pouting. That's something he's going to have to get over and deal with."

"I love you, Isabella. And thanks for always supporting me."

"You go out there and show that big city what our little town Gomer has to offer. Don't worry about anything back here. I'll talk to William."

"Thank you," she said, thankful to have a mother-in-law who had her back.

"Goodnight, sugar. Go and make us proud."

"Goodnight."

Flo disconnected the call, her heart ached, scared for her relationship and what was going through her husband's mind. William had always been her everything, her life. What would she do without him in her life? What if he can't forgive her for walking out?

She put on a big, fake smile, gathered her purse for a night out with her girls. Flo had to get her head in the game. The opponents came to devour whoever got in their way. There was no way she was going to risk everything she loved to be taken down by her competitors.

Chapter 13

The next morning, William stormed up the steps to his mother's front porch, angry that she was in on Flo's deception. Instead of knocking, he pounded on the door like a bill collector, looking for his pay. Inpatient, he began to shout his mother's name.

She opened the door, looking at him as if he'd lost his mind.

"Boy, are you crazy?" she asked mean-mugging him. "People are still asleep in this neighborhood. What's your problem?" She stood with the door wide open with her fist in a ball and a posture of someone ready to rumble.

He passed her and went inside. One thing about country folks, their business was everyone's business. Isabella flew behind him, scolding him like he'd stolen something.

"Boy, you better start talking and quick. Before I go upside your head. Who do you think you are, beating down my door like some maniac?"

William turned to face his mother, breathing hard as if he'd run a marathon. "Why are you and my wife keeping secrets from me?"

"Child, if you don't take yourself somewhere and sit down, talking that noise. I'll put a serious hurting on you."

Her slender frame strolled into the kitchen and poured herself a cup of coffee, leaving him standing in the living room. He loved and respected his mother, but today was not that day to play mind games with him. She returned and took a seat in the rocky chair he'd made for her years ago.

"Mama, I'm not for any of your games today."

She cut her eyes up at him, signaling that he'd better change his tone or else.

He collected himself, toning down the bass in his voice and said, "Why couldn't the two of you just be honest with me?" A lump formed in his throat as he struggled to keep his bruised ego in check.

While his mother sipped on her coffee all calm and proper. William knew what that meant. Isabella wasn't the type of woman who'd rush to respond to any question. When she took long pauses in between conversations, he knew she was preparing to lecture him.

"Sit down," she yelled, pointing to the recliner across from her.

As much as he wanted to stand, he honored his mother's command. William just wanted to get to the bottom of their deception. So, the sooner he sat down, the quicker she would spill her truth.

"I want you to listen and listen well." She shifted in her seat, placing her cup of coffee on the table next to her. "Your wife has been trying to share her good news with you for weeks. You closed your heart and mind to her words. You made her feel as if her dreams and desires were meaningless."

"But mama—"

She cut him off.

"Boy-yy-yy, don't but mama me." She leaned forward in her chair, causing him to sit back in his. His shoulders slouched like a little child, knowing his mother would use anything near her to throw at him.

"That's not true," he stuttered, trying to rephrase his words correctly. "I-I, didn't know how to deal with her wanting to go so far away." He buried his face in the palms of his hands, knowing that a twinge of jealousy had raised its ugly head inside him.

"Your dad would be so disappointed in you right now." She shook her head at him.

William felt so ashamed after hearing his mother's words. Unable to speak, he stared at her, wishing he could have supported his wife, instead of her getting it from others.

"Let me ask you a question, Will," she stated, putting emphasis on his name. "Have you or the kids gone into your wife's shop and looked at some of the beautiful designs she created?"

He shook his head, gesturing no.

"God has anointed your wife with an amazing gift. I bet you don't even know that people in this town and surrounding areas are wearing your wife's designs?"

A look of surprise ran across his face. He was so busy trying to make a living for his family that he wasn't aware of his wife's achievement.

"No, I didn't know mama."

"You claim that you love her, though–,"

Quickly, he cut her off before she could finish. He stressed, "I do love Flo."

"Well, you sure have a weird way of showing it. She has put her life on hold for you and them kids. Now, it's her time to put herself first. A chance like the one she's been given doesn't happen often."

He leaned forward, resting his elbows on his thigh. Hearing his mother's words ripped his soul out. Here, he thought he was being a good husband. Instead, he purposely dissuaded his wife.

"As for your question about us deceiving or withholding information from you. Son, you deceived yourself. You closed your eyes and mind to the truth that was right in front of you," she advised, rocking in her chair. "I'm your mother. And I'm not afraid to let you know when you're wrong."

Silence filled the room. His mom grabbed her coffee from off the table and leaned back into the chair. He could see the disappointment in her eyes as she stared at him. He wanted to get up and walk out, but doing so would cause him to catch a shoe in the back of his head.

"Mama, I messed up," he finally spoke.

"So, what are you going to do to fix the problem?"

"I don't know," he said pathetically, hunching his shoulders in defeat. "I haven't heard from her since she left."

"I suggest you get your head together and figure things out."

"What if she doesn't want me anymore?"

"Now, you've asked the question I have been waiting on."

"What?" He tried playing dumb, knowing he couldn't fool his mother.

"You're afraid that Flo will become successful, leaving you behind."

All he could do was drop his head.

"You ought to know what kind of woman you married. You're so busy being paranoid that you can't see the bigger picture in all of this."

He scrunched up his face and asked, "What bigger picture?"

She hissed and stared at him over the rim of her coffee mug. "You will benefit from her success too."

"I know mama. I know," he agreed, but his insecurities were telling him something different. Although he knew the truth in his heart, still, jealousy lingered close behind.

With all that was within him, he wanted to support his wife, but where would he fit into her new life?

"Your knowing is not going to fix the problem."

She left him stewing in his thoughts and headed to the kitchen, placing her coffee mug in the sink. He valued his mother's opinion but his pride wouldn't allow him to acknowledge the truth. Right now, he wanted his wife home to look after him and the kids.

Isabella strolled back into the living room, humming one of her favorite gospel songs. The last thing he needed to hear was another scolding, injuring his pride. What man in his right mind wanted his wife with four children gallivanting from state to state, chasing a dream that may or may not come true? He heard what his mom had to say about him not supporting his wife. If he wasn't supportive of her sewing, he would have never built her business next door to their home. Everyone seemed to have forgotten about that one little-known fact.

"Now, where were we?" She scratched her head, and said, "Oh yeah, we left off with you trying to make things right with your wife." She now stood in front of him, causing him to keep his guard up. "In order for that to happen, you need to stay away from that gal, Felicia."

He froze. "Felicia?" He paused, treading carefully. "What does she have to do with Flo and me?"

"Where were you last night when your wife tried calling you, huh?" Placing her hand on her slender hip, she stood flat-footed before him. "I'll tell you where you were. Out at some bar when you should have had your tale at home."

"It was not like that at all, mama," he whined, trying to justify the situation. "I went to Pete's Sports bar to clear my head after reading Flo's disturbing letter."

"You know that girl ain't nothing but trouble. Why would you give the devil room to wreak havoc in your marriage?"

"Hold up," he stopped, reaching for his mother's arm, but she yanked it away. "You're acting as if Felicia and I slept together or something."

"Then why would you go to that place if you weren't looking for something?"

"Felicia showed up as I was leaving. We were not there together."

"Well, not according to Betsy's daughter down the street. She said that homewrecker had her hands all over you." Isabella pressed her narrow finger into his chest, making known her disapproval of the situation. "You better hope Flo doesn't get wind of this."

"If Flo cared about me, she would be here," he snapped, knowing he should have kept his mouth closed.

"See, that's your problem, always thinking about your needs." Her finger now pointed in his face. "If you weren't tall as a tree, I'd knock you upside that empty head of yours."

Her face beamed red as a cooked stove as she walked off. He could see the flames igniting in her eyes. When he was a child, he knew that meant to stay out of her way or feel her wrath. He did what he should have done earlier and left. But knowing when to walk away wasn't one of his strong suites.

Feeling the need to defend himself before heading out the door, he hollered after his mom. "Inform Mrs. Messy Betsy that she and her daughter need to stop spreading lies before they end up getting someone hurt."

He charged out the door, leaving it wide open. As he stepped off his mother's porch, her nosey neighbor and daughter watched as he sped off. The heat rose up his neck to the point of flipping them off, but he decided against it. No matter what, he still had to respect his elders.

Chapter 14

An entire day has passed and no word from William and it drove Flo crazy. She tried reaching him again this morning without success. Her unanswered calls made it clear that he was upset. As hard as it was, she had to stop focusing on her troubled life back home to concentrate on winning those judges over.

Loran Sinclair, fashion guru to the stars was meeting with the five finalists later today, so Flo had to bring her "A" game to the table. She must admit though, the five designs she'd created was breathtaking. She was more than proud of her handiwork.

"Hey, Flo," Louisa said, entering the room, looking summer-ready in one of Flo's designs. "Is the small town girl of Gomer, Louisiana, ready to show these city folks what she's working with?" Her plus-size figure spun around like a ballerina.

"Right now, I'm freaking out." She sat her cell phone next to her purse, praying that William would call.

In walked Kennedy and Naydean. Her friends came dressed to impress. They looked nothing like country girls. They came to slay.

"Ladies, are you ready to take Miami by storm?" Kennedy squealed, looking fabulous in a peach, strapless dress that made her beautiful dark skin sparkle.

To everyone's surprise, Naydean dumped her old lady, frumpy outfits she usually wore. Everyone's jaws dropped at the sight of her. She wore a form-fitting red jumpsuit that was sure to have every man in town swarming around her. Naydean purchased it from one of the boutiques that sold Flo's designs.

"Wow-ww-ww," Flo sang, admiring her from every angle. "You look amazing, Naydean. I can't believe you were hiding this gorgeous figure underneath those long dresses."

"You should be ashamed of yourself, hiding what God has blessed you with," Louisa said, giving her a friendly scolding.

"I didn't want to embarrass Flo, coming to the biggest event of her career, dressed like her grandmother. So, I had to step it up a notch." Naydean stood tall and proud of her transformation and it showed.

"And that you did. Thank you. Thank all of you for having my back and wearing my designs today."

They rushed over to Flo's side, engaging in a group hug. Afterward, Naydean led them in prayer and asked for God's favor on Flo's life. They said amen, released each other and headed to the Channel Resort to unveil her work before the world-leading designers. Thankfully, she was able to bring guests with her. Therefore, her friends could share the experience with her, but it would have meant more if the love of her life was there.

The ladies stepped inside an enormous room, filled with people racing back and forth with fabric draped across their arms. There were orders being spat out by some tall, rail-thin man with his blonde hair tied up in a man bun. Whoever he was, the workers did as he said. Before Flo could take it all in, a tall, beautifully dressed, slender woman came and stood in front of them. It wasn't any woman. It was Loran Sinclair, the fashion goddess.

She proffered her hand and greeted, "Hello ladies, I'm Loran Sinclair." Her smile was tight and her voice husky, but proper. "Which one of you lovely ladies is Florence Kinkaid?"

None of them could speak. It was as if their mouths were holding their tongues hostage. After they regained their composure, Flo's tongue finally broke free. "Hi, Mrs. Sinclair, I'm Florence. But everyone calls me Flo."

She extended her hand to her idol. Mrs. Sinclair wore a beautiful black dress that complimented her toned arms and tiny waistline. Her beautiful brown skin and salt and pepper short haircut glistened under the bright lights. She never thought that a woman of Loran's stature would be so hands-on with the competition. Most reality shows that she'd watched on television only revealed the creators after the winners were chosen.

"It's nice to finally meet you. I really love the designs you submitted for the show," an enthused smile lined her painted lips. "You created an outfit for every body type, which is refreshing."

"Thank you so much." Flo tried her best to keep her excitement concealed. "These are my friends, Louisa, Naydean, and Kennedy."

She shook their hands again and said, "It's nice to meet you, ladies."

"Same here," they each said, knowing they were in the presence of greatness.

"Come," she gestured with her hand. "Allow me to take you where your set up will be on Friday." Her heels clicked against the ceramic tiled floor as they followed close behind. Abruptly, she stopped, spun around and asked, "Where did you ladies get those fabulous outfits you are wearing?"

Their eyes lit up, bright as the sun. Kennedy spoke for them, beaming with pride. "We're wearing the one and only, Flo Style Fashions." Her body twisted and turned with every word.

Flo had to admit, she was bubbling on the inside as she listened to Kennedy talk about her designs. If she had a hand growing out her back, she would pat herself on it for a job well done. She was truly feeling herself at that moment.

"Catchy," Loran said, tapping her fingernail to her lips. "I love the name." She turned towards Flo as if she'd had an epiphany. "Flo, I know that I asked each contestant to submit five designs. But I would love to have my extra models march down the catwalk, wearing these designs."

Flo cupped her mouth with her hand in shock, no doubt. "Are you serious?" Tears of unbelief and joy filled her eyes as her friends freaked out in the background.

"Ladies, I have to go. They are calling me." She turned, signaling to a young lady that she was on her way. "Ladies, have those outfits dry cleaned as soon as possible and charge the bill to your hotel account."

Flo shook her head in agreement, unable to speak from the unexpected honor of having real life, professional models wear her designs.

Like the wind, Loran Sinclair was gone.

God was truly working things out in Flo's favor. Her friends thought that they were supporting her by wearing her designs, but it was all in God's plans.

She thought the day couldn't get any better. A young, tall, blonde haired lady took them to a dressing room that housed Flo's designs. When the young girl swung open the door, the ladies stood in awe of the massive room that was fit for a movie star. The blonde turned on her heels, leaving the four alone. When they stepped inside to take in their surroundings, Flo burst into tears. This was the opportunity she had been waiting for her entire life. She knew without a doubt that she belonged there. If only her man was there, standing by her side, sharing this unbelievable moment with her.

"What's wrong, Flo?" Louisa asked, rushing to her side. "Save those tears for another day because today, you have the world at your fingertips."

Sniffling through her tears, she exclaimed. "These are tears of joy. This is more than I could have ever hoped for."

"You deserve it," Kennedy said as she wiped the tears from her eyes.

Naydean shared her thoughts. "You put in the work over the years. Now, it's your time to shine. I'm just glad that we could share in it with you."

Naydean's last statement opened the floodgates that Flo had been trying to hold since last night. She'd been trying to put on a brave face, but her heart was torn. The thought of William not answering her calls had her stressed.

Her friends gathered around to comfort her. "Flo... darling, what's going on with you?" Louisa held her hand in hers. "Those are not tears of joy."

"William won't answer my calls," she mumbled, trying hard to choke down the tears. "I can't understand why he is so angry about me wanting to start a fashion line." She hung her head between her shoulders.

Now she had upset the others with her pity party. With the tip of her finger, Louisa lifted her chin up and said, "Hold your head up high and don't you hang it low again. William loves you."

"Then why hasn't he called?"

"William is old school. He believes that it his job to provide for his family—"

"But—"

"Let me finish," Louise said while continuing to hold Flo's hand. "I'm not trying to make excuses for him. William could possibly be dealing with some insecurities or jealousy of his own."

Flo didn't buy the excuse about her husband being jealous. But she listened to what her friend had to say.

Louisa continued, "Most men believe that their wives are unhappy in the marriage when they want to start a new career, etc. And William is no different."

"I love my husband," she whined. "He knew that I wanted to become a designer since high school."

"Girl, men are not wired like women. In his heart, he knows that you love him. But his mind is telling him that you will leave him once your career takes off."

"That's stupid."

"To you, but in his mind, it's real."

Kennedy pulled some tissue from her purse and handed it to Flo. She wiped her eyes and sobered up quickly. She would try to call her husband later. For now, she needed to collect herself and get ready for the biggest moment in her life three days from now.

"Thank you, Louisa. I promise not to have another meltdown."

"The devil will find any way that he can to get you off track. Stay focused on what you came here to do. There are four other contestants hoping to win that big, fat endorsement check. Don't hand it over to them without a fight."

Before Flo could respond, her cellphone rang. She snatched open her purse to answer, hoping it was William. It was a Gomer, Louisiana number, but it wasn't William. She answered anyway.

"Hello," she answered cautiously.

"Flo?" she paused. "Hey, this is Patricia. Bessie's daughter."

"Hi, how are you?" Stunned, she covered the phone with her hand and mouthed to her friends, who it was on the phone and how did she get her number.

They mouthed back, asking Flo to find out what she wanted.

"Oh, I'm fine, girl. But you might want to keep an eye on your husband."

"What are you talking about?" Flo's hand rose to her chest, trying to remain calm.

"I saw him and Felicia at Pete's Sports Bar last night. And she had her hands all over him."

"You know how Felicia is," Flo tried keeping her voice steady. "She's always trying to flirt with him.

"I don't know where you're at, but you better not stay gone too long."

As polite as she could, Flo tried ending the call. "Thank you for your concern, but I'm unable to speak right now." She disconnected the call and broke down in Louisa's arms.

"What did Patricia want?" Naydean asked as anger staggered behind her words.

"The reason William couldn't answer my call last night was because he was out with Felicia at Pete's Sports Bar."

"What?" they shouted in disbelief.

How was she going to stay focused on the show when her man was running around town with her rival? Everyone in Gomer knew that Felicia still had a thing for William and he didn't waste any time replacing Flo with her.

Chapter 15

"Pick up," William barked into his cell phone. A day has passed and no word from his beloved wife.

"Sorry, the person you're calling mailbox is full," the recording said on Flo's phone.

Now, he was getting annoyed. He had been calling her ever since this morning with no answer. Was she purposely avoiding him? William tossed the phone on their bed. Feeling rejected, he wanted to go and hang out with the boys but decided against it. The last thing he wanted to do was run into that man-hungry, Felicia. Rumors probably were floating around town about her running up in his face at the sports bar the previous night.

A knock on the door diverted his attention from his anger. "Yeah," he hollered.

"Dad, can I come in?" Julia requested through the closed door.

"Come on in, baby girl." He pulled himself together, trying to look as if everything was okay.

"Daddy, is everything alright between you and mama?" She sat next to him, laying her head on his shoulder like she did when she was smaller.

"Ye-aa-h," he slurred. "Everything is fine. Why you ask?" Her words tugged at his heart. Truthfully, he didn't know where he and Flo stood.

"Mama left and didn't tell anyone." She stared at him and continued, "Not even you, daddy." She wrapped her arm around him, holding on to him tightly.

"I'm not going to sit here and lie to you, baby girl." His chest rose and fell from the uncertainty surrounding his relationship and the life that he'd come accustomed to. "Your mom wanted to be a designer ever since high school. She turned down a scholarship to one of New York's top designing schools. She did it to marry me." He swallowed hard as he pulled his daughter close to him. "I pray she doesn't resent me for holding her back."

Julia began to weep and said, "Daddy, I hate myself. I never knew how passionate mom was about sewing. She wanted me to follow in her footsteps but I thought wearing homemade clothes were for the needy." Julia fell in her father's arms and balled her eyes out.

He rubbed and kissed the top of her head, acquainted with her grief. "We all are at fault for not giving your mother the support needed, especially me." William wanted to cry himself for not noticing how unhappy his wife had been. They slept in the same bed and were supposed to be soul mates, yet he missed the signs. He had to stay calm in order to support his children through the unknown.

He'd been trying to reach Flo all day. It was driving him crazy, wondering what she was doing that kept her from calling her family. His imagination had gone into overdrive, causing paranoia. Had she been sucked into the life of the rich and famous? Or spellbound by men who were more polished than he; men who have seen the world, the world that she had been begging to see?

"I just want her to come back home," she said, choking back tears.

"So do I, baby girl. So do I."

William consoled his daughter while trying to comfort himself. This was the hardest thing he'd ever had to deal with. He and his wife had fought against every odd to make their marriage a success. Felicia with her home-wrecking ways and their lack of finances in the earlier part of their marriage was a challenge. He had never met a woman who couldn't take no for an answer. Even their wedding had to be by invitation only to keep unwanted guests like her from crashing it.

He held on to one of the four precious gifts his wife had given him. For years, their home had been filled with love and kids running rampant throughout the house. Now, since his wife had left, and the kids were staying with his mom, the quietness had become unbearable. He couldn't remember a day when there was silence in their home.

"Smile," the photographer said to Flo and one of the male models who would be hosting the event.

Her friends looked on, drooling over the sexy man taking promotional shots with their friend. Who was Flo kidding? She was weak in the knees herself but managed to keep her cool.

"Okay, Flo and Franko. You guys were great. And may I add, very photogenic together," the female photographer said.

"Thanks," Flo added with a smile that couldn't be contained. On the other hand, Franko said nothing. He seemed a bit into himself.

The wardrobe glam squad dressed Flo in a sleek black dress. She couldn't believe how

Loran Sinclair's team transformed her into someone she barely recognized. She felt and looked like one of the models she'd admired in the magazines.

The photographer left them to go take photos of the other four finalists.

The media was also there to cover the competition. Cameras were flashing all over the place. She was feeling like a celebrity and the competition hadn't started yet. Flo walked to where her friends stood. They were star-struck and freaking out over the host of celebrities that were swarming around the room.

A pair of hands grabbed her by surprise, spun her around, planting a wet kiss on her cheek. Cameras were flashing crazy in their direction, nearly blinding her. She wanted to slap Franko, but instead, faked a smiled for the cameras, grabbed her friends and went to another corner of the room.

He stood there, full of himself as the media made a field day out of the situation.

They asked loads of questions that she had no answers for.

One thing she learned since arriving in Miami, everyone loved to hug and kiss in this industry. Whether they meant it or not, it was something they just did. She just prayed that if the photo hit the media and news-stands, that Franko's little stunt doesn't cause a stir in her smalltown. William would break that toothpick of a man in half with his bare hands, knowing that he put his lips on his wife.

"Flo," Kennedy squealed, "OMG, you were kissed by this year's, Peoples Magazine, sexiest man alive."

The others couldn't speak a word. They were still in awe from being in the room with models they had only seen in magazines and television.

To avoid the white elephant in the room, Flo changed the subject. Panic-stricken, knowing how messy the tabloids could be, making something out of nothing, consumed her thoughts.

"I have the rest of today free. So, after I finish with the interviews, maybe we can go into town and have some fun." What she really wanted was some fresh air to stop her head from spinning. Franko's unexpected kiss had her worried. William was going to hit the ceiling, knowing that his wife was kissed by another man.

"Now, you're speaking my language," Kennedy said, waving her arms and swaying her hips.

"Although I have loved every minute of being here, I'm so ready to get loose," Louisa said.

"Yasssssss, me too," Naydean added.

The longer they were in Miami, the more Naydean seemed to loosen up. Maybe the change in scenery was what she needed to bring out her wild side. Gomer, Louisiana, had a way of choking the fun out of a person because of its old traditional ways. With the three of them being footloose and free since school, Flo wondered how they ever became friends with her. She followed them around the school campus like a lost puppy. Flo suspected that she always wanted to break out of her shell but was too afraid of disappointing her bible toting grandmother.

Once Flo finished with her last interview, they grabbed their belongings and headed out the door to explore the beautiful beaches of Florida. First, they headed to their resort to freshen up, which gave Flo a chance to try and call home again. She prayed that William would answer. It was getting hard for her to concentrate on the competition not knowing where they stood or if she had a home to return to.

They dashed off into their rooms to get dressed, which gave Flo the opportunity to call home. She punched in William's cellphone number and waited for him to pick up. She paced the length of the room. Her imagination was getting the better of her. In her mind, all she saw was him and Felicia being intimate together. Knowing that she might have handed her husband over to her rival made her nauseous. Patricia did inform her they were spotted together. How stupid could he be going out in public with her? All types of things popped into Flo's mind. Things she never in her worst nightmares wanted to imagine. She loved her husband more than life itself, but she would kill him if she found out that he was with that woman. As a matter-of-fact, he would meet his maker if he was caught with any woman.

She really had to get a hold of her wild thoughts. William was innocent until proven insane. Flo knew that he had to be angry that she'd left, leaving only a letter behind to explain her whereabouts. Surely, he wouldn't use that as an excuse to step out on their marriage.

The bed behind her was the only thing that held her limp body as the phone rang for the seventh time. She refused to play into Satan's mind games. For all she knew, William could be out on a site at work or at his mother's house with their kids. She had to stay positive and focus if she wanted to win that coveted contract.

Kennedy hollered her name from the living room. "Flo, are you dressed yet? We are ready to go."

"I'm almost done," she yelled back, clicking the ringer off. She dropped her phone into the purse next to her and made plans to try again later tonight. She jumped from the bed, headed over to the mirror, giving herself a once over before leaving for a glorious night in town.

"Hello," William ran from the shower to answer his cell phone. Disappointment grew inside him when he saw that it was his wife calling and he'd missed her again.

Lord, this cannot be happening, he thought to himself. It is as if Satan is trying to keep us apart.

He tried calling her back, but just like the last message, her mailbox was full and he couldn't leave a message. Ticked off, he tossed the phone onto the bed. He couldn't understand why she couldn't take a second to clear her mailbox. She must have forgotten that she had a family back in little, old Gomer, Louisiana.

Chapter 16

Two days had passed and no word from his wife. William slipped on a pair of jogging pants and t-shirt and headed out to the grocery store. Since Flo had been out in god knows where living it up, there was no food in the house, leaving him to fend for himself.

Later, he unloaded his groceries on the counter and like a boulder rolling off a cliff, it hit him. Flo was on the front page of a Fashion Magazine, booed up with some guy called Franko. The cover read, "Hot off the presses. Who is the new mystery woman in Franko's life?" He snatched it off the rack, nearly ripping the pages.

"What the heck is this?" he said, trying to keep his cool at the register. "So, this is why she hasn't called home to check on her family," he mumbled under his breath.

He was so taken aback by the photo plastered at the register for the world to see that he didn't hear the cashier when she said, "Sir, your total is fifty-five dollars and seventy-three cents."

She stared at him as if waiting for him to come back down to earth. Thankfully, she didn't know him personally or it would have been obvious of what had him distracted. William threw the magazine on the register for the cashier to ring up along with his other purchases. It felt as if someone had socked him in his stomach. He wondered where her friends were while Flo was getting friendly with another man. It was clear from the picture that they were nowhere in sight. His worst nightmare had now become a reality.

He paid for his things and like the speed of lightning, pushed the grocery buggy to his truck. William tossed the bags in the back cab of the vehicle like a mad man. He held tightly onto the magazine and then sped out of the store's parking lot. He knew there was no way that he could compete with Mr. Muscles, whose lips and hands were all over his wife. He couldn't believe the gall of her posing with him as if they were a couple.

His heart caved into his chest as he eyed his wife's picture in the driver's seat where he'd tossed the magazine. Hurt at the thought of her lack of concern about what people might think back in Gomer. She sure wasn't thinking about the embarrassment that it would cause her family, especially her husband. William was so deep in thought that he'd passed the street where he lived. Once he realized his error, he stayed the course and plowed down on the gas to his mother's house. She seemed to know everything about his wife than him.

Jealousy wasn't the word to explain what he was feeling at that moment. William was downright livid. He wanted to put a serious hurting on that Franko or whatever that pretty boy called himself. He had the nerves to put his lips on his wife. It angered him that Flo allowed him to do so.

Like the drivers in the Fast and Furious movies, he cut around the corner of his mother's neighborhood like a man on a mission. His thoughts were running wild. Like, what in the heck his wife was doing and who with. He shook his head, trying to rid his mind of that home wrecker.

He whipped into his mother's driveway, jumped from his Ford-150 pickup truck, grabbed the magazine off the seat, and stormed into her house like a criminal. His mother jumped from her recliner. No doubt he'd startled her.

"Boy, you're going to give me a heart attack, busting in here like you're crazy," she yelled with her hand clutched against her chest.

William eyed the bat in his mother's hand. She'd always kept it at arm's reach for intruders. "Have you seen this?" William shoved the magazine that he had crumpled in his hand in her face.

His mother, who always had something to say about everything and everybody, chose today to practice silence.

"My own mother," he said, shaking his head. "I can't believe you."

"Yes, I know about that picture. And if you weren't so busy going into bars and hanging out with that home wrecker, Felicia, you'll be available to answer your wife's calls."

"I have been home," he mistakenly raised his voice, realizing it a little too late. Before he knew it, his mother's bat was pointed between his eyes.

"Boy, I will crack your skull, if you raise your voice at me again."

"I'm sorry mama. I'm just upset that Flo would embarrass me on a national level."

"How do you think she feels? Word got back to her that you were with Felicia." She lowered the bat, propping it against the recliner.

William rubbed his hand across his head, and said, "Lord, this whole Felicia thing is spiraling out of control." The adrenaline rush he'd been riding on earlier had drained him dry. His mother's couch offered the support his exhausted body needed. The stress of not having his wife home was taking a toll on him.

"Since I have your attention," she paused and stood in front of him.

William kept his eyes on the bat. Although he towered over his mother, he knew not to underestimate her short stature. He'd always made sure that he wasn't on the receiving end of her wooden weapon. Babe Ruth had nothing on his mother. She would score a home run upside someone's head if they'd ever tried her.

"My attention for what?" He rubbed his face. William was fatigued and infuriated. The last thing he wanted to do was listen to his mother's ranting on and on about him and Felicia.

"William, I didn't raise you to be thoughtless."

His head shot up with brows raised, he stared at her.

"If you were thinking with half the brain God gave you, you would have been on a plane the moment you realized your wife was gone."

"What?" His mother was speaking Greek to him.

"Your wife expected you, as her husband, to support her and her dreams. But what did you do? You took it for a joke. Women these days aren't putting up with any foolishness. Especially when they are passionate about something."

He wanted to come to his defense, but the bat twirling in her hand like a baton warned him against it.

"You and the kids never took the time to really focus on the clothes she created for people right here in your own neighborhood." She propped the bat on the side of the sofa and took a seat beside him. "Son, look at me."

He turned to face his mom, cringing at the second serving of advice she was preparing to dish out.

"When your father was alive, he'd go to the ends of the earth to find me."

Isabella rubbed her palms in a slow, circular motion. William knew she did so only when she was irritated at him. He found it hard to look her in the eyes. They spoke in volumes of how disappointed she was with his actions and behavior.

"Now, you can take this how you want to, I really don't care." Her left brow rose as she spoke. "But you seemed to be stuck on stupid."

"Mama," his voice rose. "I'm not a child."

"Boy, I don't care if you live to be one hundred years old, you will always be a child to me."

His nostrils began to swell from his mother's sarcastic words, but he knew better. If he ever tried sassing her, it would be his last time. His mother had old-fashioned values, where a child was supposed to stay in a child's place, even if the child was a thirty-three-years old man.

"Your wife is hundreds of miles away. And you haven't heard from her in two days. Now, you're running up in my house demanding answers to some article, as if I have them."

She rested her hand on the edge of the sofa as she continued to rail on him. William sat and waited for her to finish, so he could get out of there and clear his head.

"If you haven't figured out yet what I'm saying, let me make it plain. Get your simple behind on an airplane and go after your wife."

"Why?" he asked, standing from his seat. "She left me." He swallowed hard on his words because his heart bled from the torture of seeing his wife with another man. He missed her but was too stubborn to admit.

"Flo didn't leave you. She went to take part in a competition with hopes of meeting someone who can take her further in her career."

"What's wrong with the life she has now?"

"Did you hear anything I've said? This has nothing to do with your marriage. It's about her feeling accomplished. She is not happy and it's a shame that you're so busy chasing after a dollar for the future that you can't see it."

The commotion coming from the television caught their attention. Their eyes widened when a commercial appeared on screen, announcing that the Loran Sinclair Fashion competition would be hosted live on television. Isabella ran to turn the volume up. William followed his mother, feeling a sense of pride, although he resisted the idea of his wife's career choice.

Flo and the other competitors' faces flashed across the screen, causing her to squeal with joy. Although his wife was always a natural beauty, she looked even more stunning dressed and made up like a supermodel. The other contestants failed in comparison.

His mother jumped up and down, hitting and shouting at him as if he wasn't watching the same commercial as she. "William...William, it's Flo. Flo is going to be on television."

He remained silent, unable to partake in Isabella's excitement, as she shouted and praised God, blocking the television screen. William was speechless; mostly ashamed of the way he'd behave. Despite what he thought, Flo had the courage to go and do bigger things than he'd ever imagine.

"Boy, aren't you going to say anything? Your wife is going to be on TV," she said, slapping him on the arm. "Never in my wildest dreams did I imagine how huge this fashion competition would be."

William felt the weight of his body giving from underneath him and fell into his mother's recliner. He felt foolish. No doubt, everyone in town would be supporting his wife and he didn't even know what she actually did. Some husband was he.

Maybe it was time to take his mother's advice and jump his butt on an airplane and go support his wife. What type of man was he to allow his wife to go far away from home, alone? His heart sank in his chest, knowing that he'd failed his wife. He wasn't there when she needed him the most.

Chapter 17

"Flo, you are going to be on TV," Kennedy cried from the unexpected news that filled the room.

"We are so honored to be experiencing this moment with you, girl," Louisa said. Her facial expression said it all.

Naydean spoke no words but embraced Flo in a way she never had before. Their acts of genuine happiness told Flo that this was serious business.

No doubt, all the candidates were floored to hear the good news. Even if they didn't win, the exposure would be an added bonus to getting their designs into the hands of the right people.

"I'm just as shocked and overjoyed as everyone else." The day couldn't get any better for Flo. If only her family was there with her as the other designers. Quickly, she shook off the down in the blues feeling. They were never interested in her sewing anyway. She was there with her girls. Their support and presence meant the world to her. Still, deep inside, she knew that no one could take the place of family.

The stage was built and the models were selected for the five finalists. The creative director snapped his fingers, ordering everyone to take their places. Flo had no time to sulk. She hugged her friends and went to the area where her models and designs awaited her.

As Flo began fitting one of the models for her outfit, another female contestant came over, trying to get in her head about the upcoming competition.

"Hump, you're presenting those designs for the world to see?" A tall, razor thin, blonde-haired woman asked as she strolled by with her nose thumbed up in the air. "Is Gomer, Louisiana even on the map?"

Flo wanted to shut her down with mean and nasty words of her own. But she knew that people like her only acted out when they felt threatened. Besides, she didn't want to be caught up in any negative publicity. She learned quickly how the media could spread rumors in a matter of seconds.

One of the models came to Flo's defense. "Looks like someone is jealous," she smirked at the insecure contestant. "And aren't your rags over there?" she pointed.

"Tsk," she spat, rolling her eyes at the model and headed to her station.

The noise level was through the roof as everyone worked as if their lives depended on it. Orders were shouted from every direction and interns ran frantically when they heard them. Watching everyone rushing back and forth from every corner of the room made her head hurt, but this was the life she wanted. A tight smile sprouted on her face as sewing pins hung from her lips.

A board on the wall informed each model of which finalist they were paired with.

She counted it a blessing and an honor to have her clothing even considered being part of such a prestigious event. Her plus-sized model walked in, full of confidence and much attitude.

"So... are you the amateur they assigned me to work with?" she asked, pursing her lips.

Amateur!

"I'm the designer that you will be working with," Flo snapped, trying her best to remain professional. She had been working hard to play nice to most of the spoiled prima donna, but it was time someone cut them down a size or two. They had been belittling each contestant and frankly, she'd grown sick and tired of it. She was a human being and wasn't going to allow those giant mannequins to talk down to her. "If you don't mind, please put this dress on so I can tailor it to complement your curves."

The model rolled her eyes, showing her disapproval to be working with Flo. However, she did as she was told, but not without trying to get a rise out of Flo first. "You need me. Not the other way around. So don't get it twisted."

Flo waved her off, determined not to allow anything to upset her. The model's clothes fell to the floor, causing Flo's mouth to drop open. In all her years as a seamstress, no one has ever stood before her buck naked as she altered their clothes.

"Where are your underclothes?"

"Hump...you are country. No one says underclothes." She belted out a disgusting laugh.

"Look here Lolita or whatever your name is."

Lolita's eyes widened from the sharp tone in Flo's voice.

"You are trying my patience. Now, go put some underwear and bra on, and then we can continue. If you do not comply, I will be forced to replace you."

Lolita clutched her chest and said, "I am irreplaceable." Those words rolled off her painted plumped lips but her face spoke something else, fear.

Flo had to admit, the plus-sized model was gorgeous and filled with self-esteem. She was a natural beauty, wearing huge coarse curly hair, skin that was smooth, creamy, and flawless. Flo knew her type. She had gone to school with girls just like her. Lolita's demeaning attitude probably came from years of being bullied for being overweight. Now that she was a supermodel, it boosted her confidence and in turn, made her the bully.

Just when Flo was prepared to speak with the director to send her another plus-sized model, Scarlet, a red-headed beauty, stood admiring her clothes.

"I have been eying your designs ever since you arrived," Scarlet said, thumbing through each piece.

A sense of pride overtook Flo. All she'd wanted to hear her entire adult life was that her fashions could compete with the best of them.

"Thank you." She turned, snarling at Lolita and then back to Scarlet and said, "As a matter of fact, I was looking for another model whose personality could make my designs come alive on the catwalk. And I think you're the one."

Scarlet's deep blue eyes lit up. "I was hoping that the director paired me with you. But unfortunately, I was teamed with a dictating dragon."

Lolita didn't take her being replaced lightly. She tossed Flo's dress across a rack and broke into the worst temper tantrum she'd ever seen from an adult.

"Look here you little country bumpkin, you will never win this contest without me. I'm the headliner. Everyone is here to see me," she pointed hysterical at herself. "Not you or these other amateur designers. But me," she shouted.

Like the classy lady her mother raised her to be, Flo turned on her heels in search of the director who had security to come and remove Lolita from the area. Her ranting and raving could be heard throughout the studio trash-talking Flo's designs.

Once the uproar simmered down, Flo was paired with Scarlet and four other models to showcase her fashions on the catwalk. One thing she was not going to do was to allow a high-and-mighty washed up supermodel rain on her blessing. Without a doubt, she knew that it was by the grace of God that she was even considered to take part in such a huge event. Many would love to be in her position. And to top it off, she would be on television in two days for the world to see. The moment would be even better if her man was by her side. One thing she knew for certain; all things were possible with God.

Flo made a promise to never allow anyone to stop her from walking into her destiny. She and William both sat in church Sunday after Sunday, hearing sermons about reminding God of his Word and promises and she did just that. Now, she has finally seen the window of heaven open to her. If she blew this chance, it may never come again. In time, she knew William would come around and hopefully, trust God enough to start his business.

While waiting for the five models to put on her designs so she could tailor them to their bodies, her jaws dropped when Scarlet stepped out first. With her tape measurement around her neck and needle holder strapped around her wrist, Flo excitedly got to work.

"This dress was made for you," Flo commended. She turned Scarlet around slowly to view every angle of her curvy figure. "It complements you perfectly."

Thank you, God.

"This fabric makes me feel sexy," Scarlet smiled, rubbing her hands up and down the sides of her body. "It's soft but not too yielding."

Before Flo could start pinning the areas where the dress needed altering, the other slimmer models stepped from around the makeshift dressing room and wowed her. Happy with the models who were assigned to her, Flo got down to business, making sure that not one detail was missed.

Loran Sinclair wanted each finalist to walk the catwalk and stand with their models before the winner was crowned. It meant more pressure. She had to find something to wear so Mrs. Sinclair and the judges knew that she came to win.

Like a machine, Flo worked until each models' outfits screamed, "I came to slay." Time was winding down and in two days, her fashions would be seen by millions. Everything had to be on point. There was no room for error.

Later, she locked up her designs for the night. She gathered her purse, hoping that her friends were waiting for her outside. They were late picking her up the previous day because they lost track of time ogling and stalking the male models in the lobby.

While heading to meet her girlfriends, Flo tried calling William's cellphone, hoping that he'd pick up. She needed to hear his deep, sexy, tranquil voice which always had a way of calming her. After tonight, she would be running from sun up to sun down, rehearsing for television. Her nerves had been steady up until now. Everything was happening so fast that she hadn't had time to talk to anyone but her mother-in-law. The phone rang continually with no answer as before.

He must really be upset. She'd tried contacting him for the last two days and he'd been ignoring her calls. As hard as it was, she managed to stay focused on the positive and hoped to work things out once she returned home. She disconnected the call and tossed her phone into her handbag.

Flo wanted to breakdown and cry, but she had to remain strong. Her rivals looked for any sign of weakness among each other and she sure wasn't going to allow them to see hers.

William fumbled, trying to fish his phone from his back pocket. It had rung several times before he retrieved it. "Hello. Flo...baby." Upset that he missed his wife call again, he slammed his device against the dashboard of his truck. Using the stirring-wheel as a punching bag, William pounded into it with all his might. He wanted his wife. He needed to hear her voice. Touch her. Hold her in his arms.

He pulled off the road to gather himself. William felt as if he was losing it. He wasn't the only one who missed her. His babies were missing their mother as well.

If it was up to him, he would march down there to Florida and haul her back home. If he pulled that stunt, he'd lose her forever. It was evident that her heart was dead set about what she wanted.

He had to think of something and quick. He had to let his wife know that he wasn't giving up on their marriage. No Franko or no other man was going to take his place without a fight. They shared years of history together. No pretty boy could top that.

Chapter 18

Julia rushed down a flight of stairs, heading to her second-period class. She was excited to know that her mother would be on television. Her mom's success made her and Jr. celebrities around campus. People who never gave her a second glance now took notice of her. It didn't hurt either that her mother was an alumnus. Unlike her brother, Jr., who allowed all of the attention to go to his head, a sudden sadness crept up on her. Throughout her youth, her mother tried introducing her to sewing. Each time, she refused. Julia had no interest in sewing or wearing her mother's homemade clothes.

"Hey Juls, how do you like my new outfit?" her friend asked, spinning around the entrance of their classroom door.

"Where did you get it? I like," she said, admiring the mini-skirt her friend wore.

"Don't be silly, Juls." She lightly pushed Julia's shoulder. "You know this is from your mother's teen collection."

"Girl, you know I was just playing. You are wearing that mini-skirt. Mama would be so proud of how you are rocking it."

Her friend took a few steps back and asked, "Juls, why haven't I ever seen you wearing any of your mother's designs? If my mother could show out on a sewing machine like yours...girl-ll-ll, somebody would have to beat me out of them." She stared, waiting for an answer.

Honestly, she didn't have one.

Feeling like a fool, she tried playing it off. When truthfully, she never had an interest in what she thought was her mother's hobbies. Here she stood, ashamed that other students knew of her mother's designs and wore them, and she had no clue and never allowed a fabric of it to touch her body.

The bell rang which saved Julia from further embarrassing questions that she had no answers to. Both girls rushed inside their calculus class as her friend eyed her suspiciously. She sensed her friend knew she was lying.

"We'll finish this conversation later," her friend stated as she flopped into a seat next to Julia.

How was she going to talk her way out of this? What type of daughter was she? If she wasn't so self-absorbed with her own needs and wants, she would have taken her mother's business seriously. Today, after learning that her mother would be in one of the biggest fashion competition on television, everyone has been approaching her with questions she could not answer. She wished that she was Jr. because jocks don't care one way or the other.

As far as she was concerned, her entire family owed her mother a big apology for not taking her fashion aspiration seriously. When she arrives home from her trip, Julia had a lot of making up and apologizing to do. She had not been the supporting daughter her mom needed. At the moment, all she could think about was wrapping her arms around Flo and telling her just how proud of her she was.

Julia glanced over at her friend, who wore a smile, knowing she had to think of something quick to tell her before the bell rung.

Later, several other female students approached her outside at lunchtime, sharing their enthusiasm about her mother's big event. They expressed how proud she and her family must be, to have a celebrity in the family. Although she tried to share in their excitement, what she really wanted to do was hide her face in shame.

Abruptly, Julia left the table, faking an illness. She headed to the office asking them to call her father to check her out of school. She just couldn't take it anymore. Those girls knew things about her mother that she didn't. Many had met her mom when they bought her clothes from the local boutiques. How could she have been so aloof? She knew Flo only as her mom. Never once had she talked to her about the fashion industry or her dreams as a woman.

She sat in the front office, waiting on her ride. Julia just couldn't take the pressure of answering any more questions about what was going on with her mother in Florida when she didn't know herself.

Afterward, Isabella stepped inside the office to checked Julia out of school. She sat in agony as her grandmother and the other office workers chit chatted about her mom's rise to smalltown fame. Rolling her eyes at the women, Julia tossed her backpack across her shoulder. If her father wasn't out on an assignment, he would have picked her up. He wasn't big on idle conversation, but her grandmother had no sense of time. Julia was ready to get out of that place, the sooner, the better.

She had to put an end to her grandmother's talkfest. "Grandma, please.

Can we go already?" she whined, trying to look pitiful. "I feel awful."

Isabella turned, the look on her face told that she had forgotten Julia was standing there. "Oh my word, sweetie, I've been going on and on about your mother that I forgot you were standing there."

"Ugh-hh-hh," she moaned, rubbing her stomach.

"As always, ladies, it was good seeing you all again." Isabella waved at the office workers as she held the glass door open for Julia to pass.

"We'll be praying that Mrs. Kinkaid brings that fashion title back home to Gomer, Louisiana," a female worker yelled.

"Thank you," Isabella said.

"Feel better Julia," another worker expressed, eyeing her suspiciously.

Whatever she thought, Julia didn't care. She just needed space from the students on campus. Julia also needed to ask her grandmother more about her mother and her love for sewing. Her father was of no help. He was in the dark about her mother's passion as she was.

How could a family live under one roof and have no clue about each other? As she closed the car door, her eyes began to fill with tears. For the first time in her life, she realized that she didn't know her mother, the woman called Florence.

William called the kids to inform them that he would be working late and for them to order pizza for dinner. He breathed a sigh of relief to know that Julia was feeling better. His mother was a jewel. Whenever he or Flo needed her to step in and help with the kids, she was always more than happy to do so.

Tired from the back-breaking work to meet a deadline on a property assigned to him and his crew, William stopped and took a much-needed break.

He spotted his good friend, Devin Parker. They had been friends since high school. Football brought them together but when his family was killed in a car crash, tragedy made them closer, like brothers. His grandparents took him and his younger brother in and raised them as their own. William's home became his second home. His mother treated Devin as if she was his birth mother.

After high school, neither knew what direction they wanted to go in life, so they gave construction a try. They have been together ever since. William valued his opinion. Normally, he'd never discuss his marriage with anyone. But today, he felt lost and needed to get this burden off his chest.

"Hey man, what's up?" William asked, taking a seat next to his friend. He reached inside the small cooler he was carrying and pulled out an ice cold bottle of water.

"Man." Devin shook his head. "I'd be better when this project is over." He turned, staring over at his friend.

"I hear you." William took a big swig of water. Knowing that Devin could read him just as his wife could. He decided to come clean about his lack of support for his wife and her career.

"What's up, Will? You look as if you have the weight of the world on your back." Devin stood from his stoop, in search of his cooler. He grabbed a water bottle, took a drink and said, "Talk to me bro...what's going on in that hard head of yours?"

"I think I've messed up my marriage." William took his hard hat off and laid it next to him on the ground.

"Messed up how? You know that woman loves you."

"I don't know about that anymore." He raked a hand over his head. "She took off to Florida to participate in some fashion competition. I have been against it since the first day she mentioned it."

"Against?" He looked at William as if he'd lost his mind. "Man, are you listening to how stupid that sounds?"

"Look, I know that now." He took a deep breath, rubbed his face and continued, "I have allowed the best thing that God has ever given me to walk out of my life."

"I can't believe you allowed your ego to stand in the way of your wife wanting to better herself. I wished my wife had an ounce of Flo's ambition."

"What am I going to do?" He sounded like a wounded bird that lost its direction.

"You are going to get your behind on an airplane and go support your wife. That's what you're going to do."

"I can't leave. We're in the middle of this project."

"Project... man your wife is more important than this job."

William buried his face in the palms of his hands. He'd been so busy trying to prove to himself that Flo was wrong for going to Florida that he couldn't think straight.

Devin's voice broke into his thoughts. "Man, you have a beautiful family. Don't let the devil destroy it."

"I know—"

Devin interrupted.

"No, you don't. I bust my butt every day trying to provide a living for me and my wife. But do you think she appreciates it?"

William stared at him, wanting to answer but he didn't. He just listened because right now, he wasn't in a position to give anyone advice.

"No, she doesn't. I come home from work; there is no food on the stove. The house is filthy and she's sitting on the sofa with rollers in her hair and wearing the same housecoat I left her in when I went to work."

"Wow, man. I didn't know you were going through all of that."

"The word is, was. I filed for divorce. I deserve better. I never asked her to work. Just support me and she couldn't even do that."

"I'm sorry that I haven't been there for you, man." William slapped him across the shoulder.

"Oh, I'm happy now. But listen to me and listen good; go support your woman. If you don't, trust me, someone else will."

The image of Franko's lips and hands on his wife made him growled within. But Devin was right. What type of man was he to forbid his wife from dreaming? It sounded absurd, now that he'd thought about it.

"I hear you, Dev. I love my wife. I didn't know what I had until she left."

They headed back to work. William had a lot of soul searching to do. He could only wonder what his wife thought of him. He was her protector. His stupid ego got in the way and left her defenseless and having to go through one of the toughest challenges of her life alone.

He and his family were overdue for a vacation. A vacation Flo had wanted to take for months. Once his shift ended, William was going to purchase flight tickets for the entire family. They were going to Miami, Florida, to support his wife. She deserved better than what he had been giving lately.

Chapter 19

"Places everyone," Ms. Sinclair's voice roared throughout the studio. When she spoke or snapped her fingers, everyone gave their undivided attention and gathered in their rightful places. Flo's heart pounded like a jackhammer smashing through concrete from the pressure of it all.

And just like that, everyone fell in line like soldiers.

The claws began to surface among the contestants. For the past few days, each aspiring designer was on their best behavior. Now, it was the countdown to one of the biggest fashion shows on television and everyone coveted that number one spot. From the look on most of their faces, they would do anything to win it, even sabotage.

Loran Sinclair strutted pass each of them, laying down the dos and don'ts of the competition as the construction team erected the stage behind them. Thankfully, she covered the rules for those with thoughts of trying to destroy or steal another competitor's designs.

As those words dropped from her lips, Flo's stress level went down ten notches. Two of the finalists, in particular, expressed their dislike for her through their conversation and body language. They were nice-nasty. Whenever Loran was around, they loved everyone, but behind her back, their true color showed.

Tight-lipped, Flo stared at the tall, slender, mogul. Loran Sinclair had been her idol since she could remember. When she passed Flo's way, now changing gears to teaching on proper television ethics, she winked at Flo. Thankfully, none of the others had seen it. They were already jealous, believing that Mrs. Sinclair had deemed her the winner before the competition began.

Loran clapped her hands together in a rapid motion and said, "Let's get to it, guys and girls. We have a show to put on tomorrow. And good luck to you all."

Just as quickly as she strode in, she exited the same and everyone went back to their cattiness. Drained from all the drama, after the last dress rehearsal and walk through was over, Flo rushed to the nearest exit.

She called her friends to meet her in the lobby. Stressed and the need to release some pressure, they headed down the street to a popular spa to enjoy her last day of being just an average designer from Gomer, Louisiana. Tomorrow, her entire life could possibly change.

The women made themselves comfortable in their steam baths. With white towels wrapped around their heads, they basked in the soothing warmth of the water.

Since tomorrow would be her last day in beautiful Miami, Florida, she and her friends decided to unwind, and release the negative energy she had been exposed to earlier.

"Mmmmm, this has to be what heaven feels like," Flo moaned, releasing a hand full of water she'd scooped up. "I really needed this today."

"We all needed this. Especially after listening to you talk about those fruitcakes you have to deal with," Kennedy expressed, smiling from ear to ear with her eyes closed.

"Well, I'm not trying to pull you from your moment of utopia. But have you heard from William?" Louisa asked. Worry could be heard in her voice.

The others rose from their baths and stared over at Flo. Their eyes were filled with concern. Friends since forever, she knew better than to lie to them. Truthfully, she wanted to break down and cry, but she kept her lips from quivering. She missed her husband. Watching the other finalists there with their significant others tore her heart into pieces.

After several minutes of silence, she sat up to address the question. She noticed a tear trickling down Naydean's cheek. Flo knew then that the situation was serious. She'd tried to ignore what was going on in her marriage due to the upcoming fashion show. But now, it was time to face the truth. Honestly, she didn't know what the truth was.

"No," she said, taking her time to answer. Her voice cracked and spitting out the words seemed to suffocate her. "Each time I tried calling home or his cellphone, there was no answer."

"Has he called you?" Kennedy asked with anger in her voice. Now, she had sat completely upright from her steam bath.

"Flo, you don't think what Mrs. Betsy's daughter said is true, do you?" Naydean's lean body pressed against the side of the tub.

"I don't know." Flo shook her head. "I don't know." She had no answers as to why she hasn't heard from her husband.

"Sweetie, William is a good, decent man," Louisa added. "Don't get caught up in those lies you've been hearing. We all know Mrs. Betsy and her daughter love starting fires around town."

"I'm trying to keep the faith. Maybe I should have been a woman and spoke my truth before leaving." Doubt began to surface its ugly head once again.

"You did what you had to do. He probably would have talked you out of it, anyway." Kennedy eased back down, resting her head against the back of the tub.

"I don't think William is that weak of a man to turn to Felicia as soon as you left town," Louisa said, wiping the sweat that the steam had caused from her face. "Nope, you can't make me believe that."

"I pray that is true," Flo said.

"No...that is the truth. You should know the type of man that you are married to," Louisa scolded.

Flo leaned back into her tub with uncertainty lingering in the back of her mind about her marriage. She took in all that was said, but the fact that William hadn't called her raised some suspicions in her mind.

"Let's put a pin on this subject for now," Naydean advised. "Flo has a competition to win. And she needs to be relaxed and stress-free."

"You're right," Kennedy agreed, snapping her fingers for the hostess to bring them glasses of wine. "It's going to be a shame to waste this steam bath and the message we had earlier, for you to go into the competition stressed out."

The hostess returned with four glasses of wine.

"Let's toast to Flo's victory tomorrow," Kennedy continued.

With glasses held high, they shouted, "To Flo's victory!"

The mood in the room had turned into laughter. They were now acting like teenage girls spilling the tea about everyone and everything. And her colleagues in the contest were at the top of their gossip chain. Flo had never seen such cutthroat in her life. Everyone's eyes were on the prize, but she wasn't willing to compromise her integrity for it.

Kennedy was the first to step out of her steam bath, wrapping a towel around her body. "I can't believe that Franko guy thought that you were like the other females who were drooling over him."

"I know. When he planted that kiss on me and a cameraman happened to be there, it angered me. He planned that. I know he saw the wedding ring on my finger."

"Hold up, Flo, that Fashion magazine is sold in hundreds of stores. Including Gomer, Louisiana," Naydean added, stepping out of the tub.

By then, they all were clothed in white robes and slippers that the spa provided. They left the steam room in search of some fresh air. Their heated conversations along with the steam from the bath caused the temperature to rise.

"Oh, Lord!" Flo shouted. "You don't think William saw it, do you?"

"It's possible," Louisa answered. "That's probably why you haven't heard from him."

"What if he thinks I'm fooling around with Franko?"

"They say, a picture is worth a thousand words," Kennedy said as they sat to get manicures before concluding their spa day. "You know how this industry is. They have the ability to make a picture show what's really not there."

"I don't want the people back in Gomer to think that I'm out here fooling around on my husband."

"Don't get all worked up, Flo. The people back home know the type of woman you are." Naydean rubbed the back of Flo's hand, giving her one of her reassuring smiles.

"Yeah… anyone with good sense will know that this garbage isn't real." Louisa placed her hands on the table for the manicurist to shape her nails.

"Well, let's just hope that if William has seen the magazine, he knows that." Flo sat as the manicurist re-filled her nails, hoping for the best. Now she understood how the celebrities on the cover of the Enquirer Magazine felt when lies that she thought was truth became breaking news overnight.

Chapter 20

"Thanks, mama for coming over to help me pack the twins' clothes. Flo always took care of that."

William's mom pulled every stitch of clothing he'd pack from the five-year twins' suitcase and threw them across the bed. "Hump...Flo will serve your head on a platter if you have her babies coming to the biggest event of her life, looking unkempt."

"That's why you are here. To make sure they look good. Thank goodness Julia and Jr. can pack for themselves."

William's soul sang. He'd finally put away his medieval way of thinking, thanks to his mom and friend. Freely, he could go and share in his wife's success. It didn't matter whether she'd won or lost. To know that she had the courage to chase after her dreams despite her negative environment touched him in ways he'd never imagine.

He couldn't wait to hold his wife in his arms and tell her how proud he was of her. Because of her faith and her courage, William did something he never thought that he would ever do. He researched information about starting his own construction company.

His mom zipped up the kids' bag and left the room. In stormed the twins, each grabbing hold of William's legs.

They shouted, "Daddy, daddy, daddy."

"Are we going to be in mama's fashion show?" London asked. Her wide-set brown eyes had a way of melting his heart.

"No, I'm going to be a model," Landon shouted, determined to be heard.

"Enough you two." He pulled them both from his leg. "Others will be modeling your mother's clothes. We are going to watch and support her."

"I wanted to model," Landon pouted, folding her arms.

"Me too," London imitated her sister, looking to their father for sympathy.

"You two go run along now. I have to finish packing. Our flight leaves in a couple of hours."

"Come on, London. You heard daddy."

"I'm tired of you thinking that you are the boss." She stormed out of the room behind Landon.

William grabbed the bags that his mother had packed and rolled them out the room, down the hallway. He peeked inside Jr's room and spotted him and Julia sitting on the bed in deep conversation, so deep that they didn't see him standing in the doorway.

Julia looked as if she'd been crying. Then, William overheard her say, "We ought to be ashamed of ourselves, especially me. I'm the worse daughter ever."

"Juls, stop beating yourself up," Jr. advised, "We all bear some blame in this, but we are showing up for her now."

William kept quiet outside the door, feeling lower than dirt.

"I felt like a fool at school yesterday. Everyone knew about what was going on with mama, except me. Her own daughter." She balled her eyes out as Jr. tried to console her.

"At least, we will be there when it counts the most."

That's my boy.

William cleared his throat and walked inside the room, startling them both.

"What's going on in here?" he asked as if he didn't know.

"Julia is upset that mama is in Miami alone."

"Technically, she's not alone. She's with the girls," William said.

Through her tears, Julia snapped, "They are not her family. We should have been there with her."

"Calm down, baby girl," he consoled. He walked over to her and sat down on the bed, pulling her into him. "I agree. We should be."

"Dad, I don't understand why you didn't go with mama?" Jr. asked, waiting for an answer.

"Son, it's complicated." He rubbed the back of his son's head and with the other arm, he held on to his daughter. "Let's just say that I was stupid. But I promise to make things right."

"My heart breaks that I'm her oldest daughter. And I didn't have a close enough relationship with mom to know her heart. Her passion. What drives her as a woman?"

Unable to stop his own tears from falling, for the first time since Flo had left, he allowed himself to be vulnerable and wept. Jr. moved closer to his father and held on to him.

"Baby, stop blaming yourself. You are a teenager, who is coming into her own. Your mother understands that. I'm her husband. It's my responsibility to hold her down."

The three sat on the foot of the bed, comforting one another. The twins could be heard in the other room playing and laughing.

He was happy that they weren't old enough to know what was going on. He was also glad that his mother and best friend got him to see the light. That he was selfish in wanting Flo to put aside her dreams just to make him happy.

After a long period of silence, he cleared his throat and said, "We need to get the luggage in the car so we can get to the airport on time."

"Let me go find grandma and start loading the car," Jr. said, giving his dad a hug before heading out the door. "I love you, dad."

"I love you too, son."

Julia continued to lean on her father. William could see that she was truly heartbroken and decided to stay with her a while longer. With the tip of his finger, he pulled her chin up to face him.

"Juls, I don't want you beating yourself up. What is done is done. Your mother will never hate you."

Silence held her tongue captive.

"We can't do anything about the past. But we can do something about it now."

"Daddy, I'm her daughter. I should have paid more attention to my mother. I called her clothes homemade and refused to wear them."

"You mother will never hold that against you. When we get to Miami, you can tell her how you feel. Now wipe your tears, we have a fashion show to attend."

He smiled, kissing her on the forehead.

"I love you, daddy," she said, giving him a big hug before going to finish packing her clothes.

Once William saw that his daughter's spirit had lifted, he left to finish some last minute packing. He bore a lot of the guilt himself. William could relate to his daughter's pain. Never in his wildest dreams would he have thought that Flo was serious about entering the contest. He promised himself to never take light anything that concerned his wife. If it was important to her, then it would be important to him, even if she wanted to fly to the moon, he would be right beside her.

Later, they arrived at the airport and boarded the airplane. His younger twins were acting up as always. His mother gave them the evil eye, causing them to sit up in their seat and behave like little angels.

Finally, he was in his seat. His mother must have sensed how tensed he was because she patted him on the leg, assuring him that everything would be okay. The airplane shot up in the sky, taking him on a search and rescue mission to reclaim what belonged to him.

Chapter 21

Flo isolated herself in her room the entire night. Miami had lost its magic. Homesick and missing her family had her ready to pack up and head back to Gomer. But even in her longing, Flo knew she had to finish what she started. Whether her family approved of her decision to come to Florida or not, this was a calling she had to fulfill.

After dinner with the girls earlier, she decided to call it a night. She wanted to be well rested, knowing that the cameras would capture the tiniest of flaws. She couldn't help but wonder if William knew that her designs would be televised the next day. Knowing her mother-in-law, Isabella would make sure that he received the message.

Hopefully, she'd make them proud.

She swept her hair inside her bonnet and prepared for bed. But not before giving

God, His due praise. Flo knelt beside her bed, feeling heavy from the weight of the competition and the uncertainty of what she would be returning home to. It bothered her that William hadn't tried contacting her after she'd called home so many times.

Does he still love me? she languished.

It would destroy her if she returned home to find that he had moved out. What was she going to do? She tossed that thought from her head. One thing she knew about her husband; he was no coward, except when it came to challenging himself to believe the impossible.

Tired and afraid of the uncertainty surrounding her marriage, Flo rested her face in the palms of her hands. She needed faith, that crazy faith that removes every doubt. Flo needed her Heavenly Father to wrap His loving arms around her and comfort her through the storm she was about to face.

With trembling lips, she whispered, "I need you, Lord."

She lifted her head, pressed her hands together and prayed.

"Heavenly Father, I thank you for the opportunity that you have given me. I praise you. I magnify your holy name. You are God and there is none other like you. The psalmist said, "I have been young, and now I am old; yet have I not seen the righteous forsaken, nor his seed begging bread."'

She stopped and raised her hands towards heaven, praising God. Tears chased after the other as she poured her heart out to God.

"Lord, I pray that you sustain my marriage. Please forgive me if I didn't handle things in the right way. Strengthen our love for one another. I ask that you give us the ability to work past our disagreements and obtain understanding. I need you Lord like never before."

She rocked back and forth on her bended knees, allowing the Holy Spirit to have His way and commune with her.

"Father, I ask that you be with me in the competition tomorrow. When the adversary tries to shoot his fiery darts at me, give me the ability to stand on your word. Bless my designs, Lord. Bless the models who will be modeling them. Have your way. You gave me this gift and I know that I'm not here at this appointed time by accident."

Flo wrapped her arms around herself as she continued to pray.

"Lord, this is my season. I have waited so long for this moment. Whether I win or lose, I thank you for this opportunity. In the name of Jesus Christ, I pray, Amen."

Still, on her knees, she fell forward, laying her head on the bed, thanking God over and over, reciting the twenty-third number of Psalms.

"The LORD is my shepherd; I shall not want. He maketh me to lie down in green pastures: he leadeth me beside the still waters. He restoreth my soul: he leadeth me in the paths of righteousness for his name's sake. Yea, though I walk through the valley of the shadow of death, I will fear no evil: for thou art with me; thy rod and thy staff they comfort me. Thou preparest a table before me in the presence of mine enemies: thou anointest my head with oil; my cup runneth over. Surely, goodness and mercy shall follow me all the days of my life: and I will dwell in the house of the LORD forever."

The weights from stress and doubt that had her bound were released. If only she had taken the time from her busy schedule before now to talk to the Lord. Her thoughts would have been much clearer.

Feeling her best since arriving in Miami, Flo got up from the floor and slid into bed, pulling the covers over her. Before retiring for the night, she checked her cellphone for any missed calls or messages. Sadly, there were none. But she wasn't going to allow that to ruin the best spiritual experience she'd had in a while. Flo began strolling through her phone and found that her mailbox was full, which explained why she hadn't received any voicemails. Still, it didn't excuse William from texting her.

Before she allowed the devil to steal her joy, Flo turned off the lamp. Everything was in God's hands. He would work things out on her behalf.

Forty-five minutes before their plane landed gave William a sense of relief. Everyone was asleep, except him. He had only one thing on his mind; to scoop his wife up in his arms and beg for forgiveness.

He laid his head back on the headrest, closed his eyes and prayed that there was still hope for him and Flo. God only knew the damage he'd done by not supporting the best thing that He had ever given him. He and Flo weren't on the best term when she left. Him trying to strong-arm her into staying in Gomer was a bit extreme. Like a supportive husband, he should have given his beautiful wife his blessings to spread her wings and fly. Instead, he clipped them, causing her to leave home wounded and unsure.

As hard as it was, he tried his best to control himself. Although he knew that God had forgiven him for his stubbornness, he now had to forgive himself. It was his responsibility to build up his wife, but instead, he used hurtful words to tear her down. He squirmed in his seat at the thought. So much so, that it caught his mother's attention.

"You alright, son?" she asked, eyeing him over her reading glasses.

"Yes. I'm just searching for some leg room...that's all."

Truthfully, he was beating himself up in his mind. The thoughts of how he behaved toward his wife the past couple of weeks made him ill.

Instead of continuing to beat himself up over things he could not change, he called on God for help. This by far was the worse situation he'd ever been in since he and Flo were married. He allowed his body to relax, closed his eyes and silently prayed to the Father.

Lord, please have mercy on me. Give me the opportunity to make things right with my wife. Because of my lack of faith to chase after what I want in life, I tried to stop Flo from doing what I couldn't.

Like any good mother, who could detect when her son was hurting, Isabella reached over and held his hand. Although there were no words spoken between them, her gentle touch spoke volumes to his aching heart.

William smiled, knowing in his heart that God had already worked things out. A surge of peace washed over him, giving him hope.

I thank you, Father, for loving a sinner like me. Thank you for being a God of many chances. You never held my faults over my head. I praise you, Lord. Please continue to keep me and my family together. Give me a spiritual heart to be able to hear my wife's heart.

Thank you for being such a good God. In Jesus name, Amen.

William opened his eyes to see how much longer it would be before the airplane landed. His legs shook from nervous energy. He wanted off of that plane but sadly, he still had twenty more minutes to be air-bound.

"Calm down baby," his mom advised, removing her hand from his to steady his trembling legs. "We will be there soon."

"Soon is not quick enough for me." He put his hand on top of hers still resting on his leg.

"Continue to allow the peace of God to calm you," she smiled. "Everything is in God's timing."

"I know mama. I'm just ready to see my wife."

"I know you are baby. Flo is going to be so happy to see her family in the crowd cheering her on."

His mom patted his leg and relaxed back into her seat.

William got a hold of himself and did as his mother advised; relaxed. He couldn't wait to look into his wife's big, beautiful brown eyes and plant kisses on those full, luscious lips hers.

Lord, let Your will be done.

Chapter 22

William and his family stepped out of the cab and headed into the hotel. Thanks to his mom, they were able to reserve a suite in the hotel where Flo and her friends were staying. With any luck, they would see her before the big show the next day. Since it was late and the kids were cranky from the long flight, he decided to call it a night. Besides, he wanted to be fresh and clear-headed when he faced his wife.

He carried London up to the room. For the first time since leaving home, his little busy body, the princess had finally tuckered out. Landon didn't fare any better. Jr. wrestled hard to pull her from the cab.

Although it was late into the night, Julia wanted to make a fashion statement in the city where fashion and wearing the latest designs were everything. She strolled from the car dressed in some crazy outfit that William or she could not pronounce.

His mom's quick steps had slowed. The long flight caused her legs to stiffen.

"Don't worry about me, baby. These old legs will shake back," Isabella exclaimed as she shook each leg to lessen the stiffness.

A weak smile etched across his face. Not only were the kids exhausted, but he was also. He could hear the bed calling his name.

Julia and Jr. were patrolling the hotel lobby for the rich and famous.

William headed toward the front desk to check-in. The receptionist greeted them with a hearty welcome and smile. He gave his name, pulled out his driver's license and credit card. She typed the information he'd provided in the computer. Minutes later, she handed him three key cards and wished them a pleasant stay.

A bellhop came, placed their luggage onto a luggage rack, which made it easier to carry the kids without the hassle. The elevator door finally opened, taking them to paradise. His mom got in first, and then he and the kids. Each breathed a sigh of relief to know that they were just a few minutes away from their rooms.

"Finally," Jr. expressed. The weight of his sister had worn him down.

"I need to get my beauty sleep. I have to be fresh just in case I'm seen on TV," Julia said, sweeping her natural curls back off her face.

Jr. rolled his eyes as he shifted the weight of Landon across his shoulder. "Tsk...please. Don't nobody want to see you."

"No, speak for yourself," she pointed her finger at him.

"Stop it you two," William yelped. "I know we are tired, but you two are behaving like babies."

Julia folded her arms, resting her body on the back rail of the elevator with her mouth poked out like a two-year-old. The weight of Landon was wearing Jr. down, but he managed to keep her secure in his arms.

Thankfully, their rooms were on the sixth floor. William didn't know how much longer he could go. He began to believe that bringing the kids was a bad idea, but they missed their mom just as much as he and deserved to be there.

The elevator door opened and Julia and Jr. headed out first. Taking quick steps, they headed down the hallway in search of their rooms. His mom had a room with the kids and he and Flo would share the other. That was if things worked out as he had planned. The last thing he wanted was for the kids shouting and running all over the place, ruining his make-up fest with Flo.

William didn't feel the least bit sorry for his mom having to look after the kids. Actually, he felt sorry for them because he had an old school mother. She didn't play and they knew it. As long as they were in her care, they would behave like kids who had some sense.

Since Flo informed his mom of the details surrounding the show, he knew that it would be impossible to see her before it aired. Besides, he wanted to conceal their presence there until tomorrow. So, he decided to sleep in late and then he and his family would take in the sights of Miami at noon.

"Dad-dd-dd," Jr. whined. "Do Julia and I really have to hang out with you, grandma, and the little brats?"

London's head whipped around. She and Landon locked eyes as she asked, "Who is he calling a brat, Landon?"

Landon hunched her shoulders and answered, "Must be Jr. cus he just stopped wetting the bed yes-ter-day."

Jr. looked around the hotel restaurant to see if anyone heard his sister.

"Mm-hmm must be," London agreed, pursing her lips. She stared at him from head to toe.

"And Juls know she better not say nothing."

"Who you telling," London added. "Her hair is bigger than her whole body."

"Poof," Landon sounded as she held her hands out to her head, making fun of Julia's puffy hair.

They looked over at their older siblings and began to laugh at their expense.

"Stop it you two," William scolded, turning his attention back to the eldest kids. "Who do the two of you know in Miami to be walking these streets?"

"Yeah, ya'll not grown," London barked.

"They think they are, girl." London rolled her eyes at them as she sucked up a mouth full of spaghetti.

William hated when his mom sat back and critiqued him with her eyes as he parented his kids. He knew that she didn't agree with some of his strict rules, but the dangers were far worse than when he was their age.

"But dad...I don't want the ladies to see me being led around like a child. I'm sixteen-years-old."

Before William could speak a word, his mother finally broke her silence, giving her thoughts on the situation.

"Will, loosen the reins," she urged. "We didn't fly all the way to this beautiful city not to enjoy ourselves."

William wasn't afraid of what his kids might do. He was afraid of what some sick individual would do to his naïve kids. Watching the evening news and the heinous crimes they aired made him scared to venture out into his own backyard. But as hard as it was, he did as his mother advised.

"The two of you can go, but meet us back at the hotel soon and don't be late, understood?"

"Thank you, daddy," Julia said, kissing him on the cheek.

Jr. gave a two-finger salute at his dad and scooted from his seat.

"I mean it, you two. We have to get dressed and be on time because once the cameras start rolling, no one will be allowed to enter the taping of the show.

"Understood dad," Julia said, leaving to join her brother.

William watched as they headed out of the restaurant, praying that the Lord would watch over and protect them. He knew they were practically adults, but knowing that doesn't make it any easier. They came from a town of innocence and he didn't want his children to be gobbled up by the evils that plague many big cities.

"They are good kids, William," Isabella said. "You and Flo raised them to be responsible."

"Thanks. It's just that there is so much out there to get into."

"Baby, you have to pray and hand them over to God."

"I know mama. I know." He tried to finish his meal but couldn't. He looked over at his five-year-old twins, knowing in a couple of years, he'd be right back in the same position.

Chapter 23

Flo was a bottle of nerves. Today was the day and for the first time in years, she was unsure of herself. The dry cleaners delivered the outfits they wore when they first met Loran Sinclair. She loved them so much that she wanted the extra models to strut down the catwalk, wearing them.

She requested that the celebrity hairstylist who would be doing her hair later for the show knew how to style natural hair. If not, one of her friends would have to step in. She'd worked too hard after cutting the perm from her hair, to allow some inexperience stylist damage her natural locks. On a last minute whim, Flo decided to remove her sew-in and be her natural self for the event.

As Flo played with her hair in the mirror, she couldn't help but think that she'd seen Jr. and Julia walking near the beach area. But she quickly tossed it from her mind and assumed that she was just missing her family.

"Girl, are you ready to go take what's yours?" Kennedy waltzed in her room, looking like a million bucks.

"As ready as I ever will be." She removed her outfit from the plastic, placing it on the bed.

"Well, you need to start getting dressed. I don't want Mrs. Sinclair to have a stroke when one of her protégé shows up late."

"Oh, trust me… she won't be cracking the whip on me."

They laughed as Kennedy strutted out of the room.

When her door closed, giving her privacy, Flo stared at her hands. They were shaking out of control. She thought it best to say a small prayer before leaving. If the Lord didn't calm her down and fast, she just might stumble and fall when the finalists take the stage. The last thing she wanted was to be the laughing stock on social media and across the world. One thing about people, they never forget.

She busied herself, being careful to choose the right accessories to complement her outfit, making sure that she looked as if she belonged on that stage. Maybe she should get one of her friends to help because it was hard for her to decide what went with what. Her nerves had her matching colors that clashed with her outfit.

"Lord please, calm my nerves. I want tonight to be perfect. And if William and the family can't be here with me, at least they can see me looking my best on television."

Flo sat on the edge of the bed with her elbows on her thighs and hands resting on the sides of her face. She had to get herself together because her stress level was so high to the point it caused her to develop a migraine.

Before she could fall back on the bed, her cellphone rang. "Hrrrrrrrr," she growled, knowing that meant she had to get it off the lampstand. As hard as it was, she pulled herself up to answer it. "Hello."

"Hey baby," Flo's mom greeted, excitedly.

"Hi mommy," she squealed, knowing that she needed to hear a familiar voice from home right about now.

"Although I can't be there to cheer you on because of my condition, I will be screaming at the television."

"Mama, this is a dream come true. Never in a million years did I think that this day would come." A tear trickled down the side of her face.

"I'm proud of you, sweetie because you never gave up."

She could hear and feel her mother's love through the phone. Flo wished that her mother and family could be there with her. It would be the icing on the cake, the big finale to a beautiful night.

"How are you doing, mama, since the doctor put you on a new medication?"

"We're not talking about me. The question is how are you doing?"

From the sound of her mother's voice, she was getting ready to start fishing around in her business. The last thing she wanted to discuss was her marriage. She assumed that William had made his decision. No text, no calls meant that he didn't want her. This was her time to shine, to prove to the world that she was a great designer.

"I'm doing great," her voice went up a notch, hoping to fool her mother.

"Girl...cut the act. This is your mother you're talking to. I can hear that something is wrong in your voice."

The last thing Flo wanted was to get bombed out, bringing her stress level even higher than what it was before. Her mother wasn't the type of woman who took no for an answer, so Flo knew she had to start talking.

"Oh mama," she whimpered, trying to keep from crying but she couldn't.

"Let it out, baby. I wished I could be there to hold you in my arms."

"He doesn't love me anymore, mama." She rubbed her nose with the back of her hand.

"Yes, he does. That man would fight to the death to be with you and those kids."

"If he loved me, why hasn't he called or texted me?"

"Well, why haven't you called or texted him?"

"I've tried, but he would never answer. And with the rehearsals and everything, I had to keep my phone off throughout the day."

"William adores you, Flo, and you can't make me believe otherwise. It's just miscommunication between the two of you."

"I hope you are right, mama. But it still does not excuse him for not reaching out to me. And to make matters worse, I keep hearing rumors of him and Felicia being seen together."

"Girl, now you're talking like a fool. William doesn't want that nasty girl. You better stop listening to all that garbage."

"But Mrs. Betsy—"

Her mother cut her off before she could utter another word.

"I don't want to hear anything about that mess pot or her daughter. That's all them two do. Sit on that front porch, spreading lies about what's going on in other people's lives."

Flo rubbed the back of her neck, wondering how her life had spiraled out of control. Her mother was right about Mrs. Betsy and her daughter. Yet, she allowed it to get the best of her.

"You're right."

"I know I'm right."

She could hear, I told you so in her mother's voice, but Flo had to admit, her mother was right when it came to no good people.

"I didn't call to beat up on you, darling. I want you to go out there tonight and show those fashion people that something good can come out of little, old Gomer, Louisiana."

"Thank you, mama." She felt better already and was happy that after tonight, she would be heading home.

"Now, go out there and give them hell."

"Mama!" she yelled into the phone.

"Whatttttt," she sang."

"When did you start cursing?"

Flo never heard her mom say a bad word in her life. She taught her at an early age that a good man didn't want a woman with a foul mouth. She was the epitome of primed and proper and taught her likewise.

"Just now."

"I'll let that one slide."

They laughed.

"Well, baby you go on now and get yourself beautiful. The ladies and I back home will be cheering for you."

"I love you, mom. Thanks for calling. I needed that."

"I love you too, baby."

Later that evening, Mrs. Sinclair sent an entourage to escort her and the other contestants to the event. It was first class treatment like she'd never seen before. Now she knew how celebrities felt, except they didn't have anyone screaming for their autographs.

Awaiting her was a platform that could possibly take her designs straight to the top.

William, the twins, and Julia rushed inside the elevator to head to their rooms to get ready for Flo's event. His mother and Jr. had already made their way to the rooms earlier. The door closed before they could see what all the commotion was about. He assumed it was some celebrity everyone was fussing over.

"Dad dd-dd," Julia whined, looking at her reflection in the mirror of the elevator. "I missed seeing another celebrity."

William was so excited about surprising his wife today that he drowned out his daughter's whining. The only celebrity he wanted to see tonight was his wife, in his room and hopefully in his bed.

Chapter 24

"Everyone, take your places," the director yelled, snapping his fingers backstage. "It's time for the show to begin." He spun around on his heels, disappearing from view.

Flo and the four finalists were shaking like leaves. The roars from the studio audience could be heard backstage, which caused more anxiety. The contestant and their assigned models were sectioned off in the order they would be strutting down the catwalk. Each wore their poker face, but truthfully, it was a façade to psych the opponents' out. No one there had nerves of steel. Flo relied on prayer and her faith to get her through tonight.

Franko brushed passed Flo, giving her a wink when the announcer introduced to the audience that he would be the MC for the show. If it wasn't the most important moment in her life tonight, she would tear into his self-absorb behind. The problem was that he'd never been told no by a woman. If his advances continued after the competition, she planned to give him a good old country beat down. Flo couldn't deny that he was a very attractive man and had a body to match. Unfortunately, it turned her off when a man was more into himself than the women he pursued.

A big screen television came on backstage, giving them a glimpse of what was taking place out on the stage and in the audience. The camera made sure to focus on every megastar among the crowd. Never in her wildest dreams had she imagined that the competition would be such big news. Flo envisioned that she would come to Florida, show off her designs and head back home. But, it had turned into something so much more.

Many nights she stayed up and cried because no one believed in her. She had to meditate and call on God in order to stay encouraged and from losing sight of the bigger picture. This moment made every hurdle she'd had to jump over, worth it. She was finally getting the recognition she deserved.

Whatever Franko was saying on stage, the crowd was under his spell. The television backstage was on mute. She guessed to keep them from being distracted or discouraged if something negative was said about them or their designs.

The five of them stood in a single file line as the backstage coordinator prepped them one last time on what to do and where to stand when their names were called. As the coordinator spoke, Flo had to take deep breaths to keep the blood from rushing to her head. It would be an embarrassment to come this far only to pass out in front of millions of watchful viewers.

She gave herself a once over and waited for her name to be called. She prayed that Franko would behave himself and not lead the audience on that something was going on between them. Social media was doing enough damage control itself about that kiss. It was spreading like wildfire that maybe she was his new love interest. Now, she understood how the tabloids took lies and made them into juicy stories. Sadly, it didn't take an entire month to print garbage. Apparently, news-worthy stories could be cranked out in a matter of minutes with new technology. She was a married woman whose wedding ring could clearly be seen in that staged, meaningless kiss.

When Flo heard her name, she tugged at the black, skin-tight jumpsuit that accentuated every curve imaginable. She had to admit; the top complemented her elongated neckline and a small amount of cleavage showed as she strutted onto the stage as if she owned it. Taking her place alongside side the four other designers, Flo smiled, as her eyes danced around the audience, being careful not to look too anxious. She did as she was coached during the earlier rehearsals.

The lights were blinding, making it impossible to recognize anyone in the crowd. She knew her friends had to be somewhere amongst the audience. Then her mind switched gears, turning to William and the kids. She prayed that they were watching. Instead, of dwelling on the negative, she was thankful to share the experience of a lifetime with her close friends. Their faith in her creative abilities never wavered since childhood.

After they were introduced to famous designers and the viewing audience, Franko hit them with a shocking revelation.

"Ladies and gentlemen, we are shaking things up a bit for our second annual fashion event," Franko announced, soaking up the limelight. "Last year, we had a panelist of our peers as judges. But tonight's winner will be chosen by our viewing audience."

A hush fell over the room.

Like a pro, Flo continued to smile, while crumbling apart on the inside. Unlike her, being able to stay poised after hearing the turn of events. Two of her opponents were heard mumbling under their breaths.

Once the heavy blow was given, they were directed off stage to dress their models for the catwalk. One of the finalists voiced his disapproval of the change while walking off the stage. Needless to say, it didn't sit well with people who had the power to make him or break him.

"Regular people?" he scoffed, tossing his scarf over his shoulder. "Who knows nothing about fashion, will be judging my designs. How undignified of them. My future is in the hands of amateurs." He strutted towards his area, mumbling words she wouldn't have dared repeated.

It was time for lights, camera, and action. She adjusted herself after hearing the turn of event. Flo sprang into action, trying to win the viewing audience over. She'd hone her craft for years. Now, it was her time to come out of her little shop in Gomer, Louisiana, and show the world her creations.

To see her clothes on the backs of the world's top models, made her feel like a proud mama. Their sizes ranged from a zero to plus size. Thankfully, she knew how to tailor her outfits to complement each body type.

Nosey, she peeked over at her rivals and saw that one was arguing with the models. A few had a hard time getting it together. The change in events had rattled them, but they were making things harder than it had to be. She heard screams from a model being poked with a pin and another threatened to never work with amateurs again. Thankfully, things were going her way. She turned and smiled at the group of young ladies and male models she was given.

With her hands in a praying position, she whispered, "Thank you."

The models were ready to zoom into action. With smiles on their faces, they readied themselves to showcase Flo's designs. Gratitude filled her heart for the gift God had anointed her hands to create. Knowing that she took something from nothing to produce a masterpiece gave her sheer satisfaction.

William's chest swelled with pride after seeing his beautiful wife, owning the stage. Without a doubt, he knew she was in her element. He wasn't too happy that he had to watch the man, who'd kissed his wife host the show, but he had to endure it somehow. If the room wasn't filled with cameras and witnesses, he'd walked up there and put a serious hurting on him.

The twins pulled on his suit coat, whining that they had to go use the bathroom. Thankfully, the cameras stopped for a commercial break. He hoped they would be quick because he didn't want to miss seeing his wife and the designs she invented.

"Come on, daddy, before we go on ourselves," London sang, looking up at him as they both squirmed.

Asking Julia or his mother to take them was out of the question. Their faces told him that they were not budging from their seats. Jr. was out of the question. With all the beautiful models and female stars roaming around the place, he might end up losing them or getting lost himself. As hard as it was, he pulled himself up from his seat, grabbed their hands, and led them to the nearest family bathroom.

The kids were bouncing all over the place after having to sit still for over an hour.

They'd made their way to a bathroom not too far from the door they had exited from. Thankfully, there were no lines due to the genius who built the bathroom with numerous stalls.

"Hurry up so we don't miss mommy," he urged, pushing them inside the stalls next to each other. He wouldn't dare leave them unattended, knowing the mischief they would cause.

Landon opened the door and asked, "Daddy, can you help me loosen my button?" She danced in place as he fumbled with the button.

William hurried and got the button free. "Now hurry. We have to get back." He gently pushed her back into the stall.

He rubbed a hand over his head in frustration because he didn't come all the way to Miami not to see his wife make her debut as a designer.

To his surprise, they both jumped out of the stalls and sang, "All done, daddy."

"Great... now let's go wash your hands and get back inside."

"Yeahhhhhhhhhh, we're going to see mommy," London screamed as the water ran over her hands.

William handed them both some paper towels to dry their hands and rushed them out. As soon as the door swung open, there appeared Louisa, Kennedy, and Naydean.

"William," they screamed.

They ran over, hugging him and the kids.

"Flo is going to be so happy that you came," Louisa shouted, holding onto him as the others released his embrace. "She thought you didn't love her anymore."

"What?" He shouted as he held onto his kids' hands. The kids tried breaking free to go with them.

Naydean and Kennedy expressed their excitement of seeing him but urged that it was time to head back inside before the cameras began to roll.

I have a lot of kissing up to do after this show. I really messed up this time, he thought as they went their separate ways.

Chapter 25

William watched from his seat as the models who wore Flo's designs gracefully took the stage one after the other. Oooo's and ahhh's took over the room. He never pictured himself ever watching a fashion show, but he found it quite interesting. Aside from the excitement, Louisa's words continued to torture him. Thankfully, he'd put his best foot forward earlier to surprise his wife. He'd purchased a dozen roses and paid security a hefty tip to have them delivered in his wife's dressing room before the competition ended.

Designers in the audience stood to their feet when the last model left the stage. They loved his wife's designs. He pressed a hand to his lips and smiled. Their enthusiasm was contagious, causing everyone to join in.

Once applauds faded, Franko appeared back on the stage and said, "We've seen some amazing talents here tonight. Now America, we need you to cast your votes for your favorite designer. This year, we have up the first place award to five hundred thousand dollars."

The audience screamed at the amount.

"Daddy," Landon whispered, "Is mama going to win?"

"I hope so baby. But it's up to America."

"Well, America better vote for my mama," London said, causing others to look their way and smile. "Shhhhhh," William put his finger to his lips.

On cue, the twins sat back, poked out their lips, and folded their arms. He had to keep them on separate sides or face being kicked out because of their antics.

"The winner will be announced later on in the show. Meanwhile, we have the Grammy Award-winning band, Treasure, here tonight," Franko announced.

William needed to step out for a second for some fresh air. The stress of not knowing the fate of his marriage was getting the better of him and the kids had gotten on his last nerve. He got his mom's attention and asked her to watch them. He left just when the band began to play.

The tension behind the stage was thick. Everyone had their eyes and daggers on Flo. It wasn't as if she made the audience give her designs a standing ovation. Her models were the ones who made them come alive.

Lord, it's in your hands. Let Your Will be done.

Butterflies had filled her stomach. She and the others would know the outcome soon. Instead of dwelling on winning or losing, she decided to savor the moment. Whether she won or lost, the memories of that day would forever be with her.

In the midst of her thoughts, Flo heard a disturbance coming from the back entrance, where no one was allowed to enter. She prayed it wasn't some crazy person trying to force their way inside to hurt anyone. With mass killings, hate crimes, and terrorism on the rise, one had to keep their guard up.

The noises finally stopped, and she turned her attention back to the television. Waiting for the band to complete their three sets took an eternity. Too nervous to sit down, she stood with her arms wrapped around her. Without warning, she felt the presence of someone standing behind her.

Lord. She rolled her eyes, knowing what was about to go down, ruining her big moment. *If this is Franko, I will slap the taste out of his mouth.*

Before she could turn to see who the mysterious person was, a pair of hands enclosed around her waist. Angry and fed up with Franko overstepping his boundaries, she turned and smacked him in the face.

"Didn't I tell you that I was married you piece of–"

In total shock, she cupped her mouth with her hands.

"Shut up and kiss me, woman."

"Will...William! How...why, what are you doing here?" her words rushed from her lips. She leaped into his arms and did as he'd asked.

Their lips parted. Each stared at the other in disbelief.

"Flo, I am so sorry for not believing in you. I promise this day forward to stand by your side."

He peeled her from his arms.

"You came, baby, that's all that matters to me." Tears of joy filled her eyes. God had answered her prayers and nothing else mattered at that point. She had a promising career and a man who showed his love by chasing after her.

"I'm so proud of you, darling." He pulled her back into his arms. "You did what I didn't have the courage to do. You went after what you wanted." He kissed the tip of her nose.

She scrunched up her face and asked, "Was that you causing the ruckus outside?"

"You darn right, that was me." He kissed her forehead. "I was prepared to pull the hinges off the doors if those big brutes wouldn't have let me in."

"And they just let you walk in?" She found that hard to believe.

"Enough about how I got in. Thank you for not hating me. I have to admit that I wasn't the supportive husband that I should have been."

She pressed her finger to his lips to silence him.

"You're here now, which speaks volumes of the type of man you are." She reached up and kissed him and said, "As far as I'm concerned, all is forgiven."

Everyone backstage stared at them, although they had no clue what was going on.

Franko walked passed them to take the stage. He knew better than to make any advances toward her now. William's eyes said just what she was thinking. If he wanted to live to host another show, he'd better stay far away from her.

The band had finished their performance, now it was time to announce the winners.

The coordinator called for the five finalists to take their places on stage when their name was called. Flo turned to her husband, feeling like a bird that had gotten its wings back.

"It's in God's hand," he encouraged. "I'll be right here when you return," he pointed where he stood.

She jumped in his arms, holding on to him tightly.

"Places everyone," the coordinator shouted again.

"Go on baby, it's your time."

"America has spoken," Franko announced, flashing his million-dollar smile at the crowd. "You have seen their designs, now it's time to see who America has picked to walk away with a contract to Elite Fashions worth five hundred thousand dollars."

Flo swore she heard her knees knocking and teeth chattering in her mouth. It was the most nervous she'd been since the competition began.

Not a sound was heard in the audience. Every eye was on the envelope Franko held in his hands. "Again, we have another twist in the competition. I will announce the person with the lowest to the most votes. As I call your names, please leave the stage. There will only be two left standing to battle it out for this coveted spot of America's Favorite Designer."

Franko turned, and pointed at each contestant, slyly winking at Flo, which she pretended not to see. If he knew better, he'd keep his eyes on the teleprompter. Even after seeing her and William together, he still had the audacity to flirt with her.

He spun back around to the audience.

He called one name after the other. Each time she held her breath, waiting to take her exit off stage. She became oblivious of everything that was happening around her. At the sound of the last name being called and her senses came back to her, there she stood next to the finalist she least liked.

"America has spoken," Franko declared, waving the cue cards in his hand toward Flo and the man she prayed to beat. "But before we feel sorry for the runner up... he or she will be leaving tonight with fifty thousand dollars."

Can you just get on with it? Her shoes had begun to hurt her feet and she had some serious making up to do with her husband.

Not only was the crowd on pins and needles, but she as well. It had been a long day and now she was ready for it to end. How celebrities go and go and go was beyond her.

This was her first professional event and it had taken its toll on her.

No matter what was going through her mind, Flo kept a smile plastered on her face, praying that her name was called.

The panelist of designers sat frozen in their seats. Some hands were clasped to their lips, while others had impatience written on their faces as Franko savored his time in the spotlight.

"Ladies and gentlemen, the winner of the second, Fashion Competition is…"

Finally.

"Florence Kinkaid," he shouted.

Two female models came and escorted her rival off stage, minutes after her name was called. Sore loser shone in his demeanor.

Shock and surprise aren't the words to describe her emotions. Her hands covered her mouth as tears of joy streamed down her face.

Loran Sinclair made her way to the stage to present Flo with her award. She announced that Flo's designs modeled tonight would be in department stores by the end of the year.

Franko tried making his move one last time before leaving the stage. Being as brazen as he was, he tried congratulating her with a kiss. This time, Flo was able to avert it with a quick handshake.

"Young lady, do you have any words for our audience and everyone in TV land?" Loran asked, handing Flo the microphone.

"I would like to thank, my Lord and Savior, who blessed me with this gift. America, thank you for loving my designs enough to vote for them. I also want to thank my family and friends for being here tonight."

She heard her kids yelling and screaming, "We love you, mom."

She responded, "I love you too. And thank you, Mrs. Sinclair, for putting on a show as grand as this to shine a light on the undiscovered talent around the world."

Flo waved and blew a kiss out to the audience. A young lady came and whisked her away where a beeline of reporters awaited her backstage.

She never expected after leaving home a few days ago that she would walk away with a contract with Loran Sinclair and five hundred thousand dollars. It wasn't easy leaving her family to chase after a dream, but she couldn't have lived with herself if she didn't. She could truly say with conviction that she went, she sought, and she's conquered.

Chapter 26

"Mommy, mommy," the twins screamed, running toward Flo.

The rest of her family caught up with the kids as they surrounded Flo with congratulations.

With arms outstretched, she eagerly embraced her youngest kids. "My sweet babies," Flo squealed, kissing them nonstop.

"Mama, we are so proud of you," Julia said, reaching over the twins to hug her mother.

Jr. tugged at his imaginary chin hairs and asked, "Mom, is there any way you can hook me up with one of those sexy models wearing your clothes?"

"Boy, what do you know about sexy?" William asked, playfully pushing the side of his head.

Her friends were all speaking and singing her praises.

"Everyone, give my Fashionista some room. I haven't had the opportunity to properly congratulate her." He wrapped his arms around her, giving her a passionate kiss.

"Ee-ee-ew," Julia sang, covering her eyes as she made regurgitating gestures. "Go get a room."

"Leave your parents alone," Naydean chimed, smiling. "They haven't seen each other in days."

"Oooooo, Landon, they are being naughty," London said.

"Yeah...there are little kids in the room." Landon tugged at William's suit jacket, trying to make them stop.

Jr. didn't say a word. He was too busy eyeing every female that passed by.

A couple of passersby's congratulated Flo and told her that America made the best choice. Kennedy couldn't help but voice her opinion. "I know that's right." She was loud as always.

Isabella expressed, "Flo, I am so proud and honored to be sharing this moment with you."

"Thank you, Isabella. I just wished my mom could have been here tonight."

"You know she would if she could have. But rest assured, she was glued to the television." Isabella gave her a motherly hug and a kiss on the cheek.

"It's time we let Flo go handle her business with the photographers," William said, releasing her from his arms. "Then afterward, we are going out to celebrate. You deserve the best, baby. He kissed her. Mom, if it's not too much to ask. Could you please watch the kids tonight?"

"I wouldn't have it any other way, son"

"Yeah. You go handle your business. We will help Mrs. Kinkaid with the kids," Louisa added, giving them a wicked smile.

Flo whispered in his ear, "I will meet you later in your room, Mr."

His body language expressed what words couldn't. Giving him a tight hug, Flo left to be photographed by every fashion magazine imaginable.

Not quite out of hearing range, Flo overheard her husband say, "I don't know what I did to deserve that woman."

"You really have some making up to do," his mom said, "Yep, you dodged a big one this time. I don't know if I would have been so forgiving."

"Mom...really."

Flo smiled at their conversation as she disappeared around the corner to make her debut as the newly crowned designer in America.

William thought the interviews would never end. Now, he and Flo were finally alone. While she was in the bathroom freshening up, he busied himself, setting the mood for a romantic evening. To keep the kids from disturbing them, he'd asked the hotel manager to change their rooms.

He popped the cork on the champagne, while soft music played in the background and lights dimmed. He knew he'd messed up but was determined to prove to his wife how much he valued her.

Flo emerged from the bathroom, looking sexy as he'd remembered. Her natural curls flowed around her beautiful face. Her flawless skin glistened under the subdued lightening. Unable to resist her any longer, William made his way over to her.

"Baby, I want to thank you for not giving up on me. I know I took you for granted. But, your leaving caused me to realize how valuable you are to me."

"Will, I don't want to rehash the past. We both have our faults. I just want to move forward in our marriage." Flo swept the sides of his face with the back of her hands.

"I have a surprise." He placed her hands in his.

Her eyes widened. "A surprise," she said, hesitantly.

"When you left home, at first, I was angry."

"Is that the reason you were with Felicia?"

"Baby, despite what you heard. Know that I will never cheat on you, especially with Felicia."

"I hope not for your sake," she said, matter-of-factly, wrapping her arms around his waist.

"Nothing happened between us." He stared her straight in the eyes and spoke his truth. "No matter how angry I get, I will never hurt you in such a disrespectful way. No woman is worth losing my family over."

"Let's get back to us. I don't want to ruin the night talking about her." Flo stood on her tiptoes, planting a kiss on his lips. "What's your surprise?"

"I'm starting my own construction company."

"William, are you serious?" She jumped in his arms. "I'm so proud of you." Flo planted kisses all over his face.

"It's because of you. You made me believe in myself." He pulled her chin up toward him and gave her a passionate kiss.

As their lips parted, she whispered, "I love you, Will."

"I love you too, my queen."

Missing his wife for days, William walked her backward to the bed, while kissing her uncontrollably. Gently, he placed her on the bed and loved her as he'd never loved her before.

Their journey taught him a very important lesson. A love like his and Flo only happens once in a lifetime. He'd follow her to the moon and back just to be near her, knowing that the journey was worth the ride.

If you enjoyed reading, *Chasing A Dream*, Please leave a review at the bookseller where you purchased your copy. You can find other books by Sheila L. Jackson at www.sheilaljackson2.com or any online site where books are sold.

Contact Information

To contact Sheila L. Jackson for a book signings or speaking engagements, you can email her at: SJ@comcast.net or visit her website, hhtp://www.sheilaljackson2.com